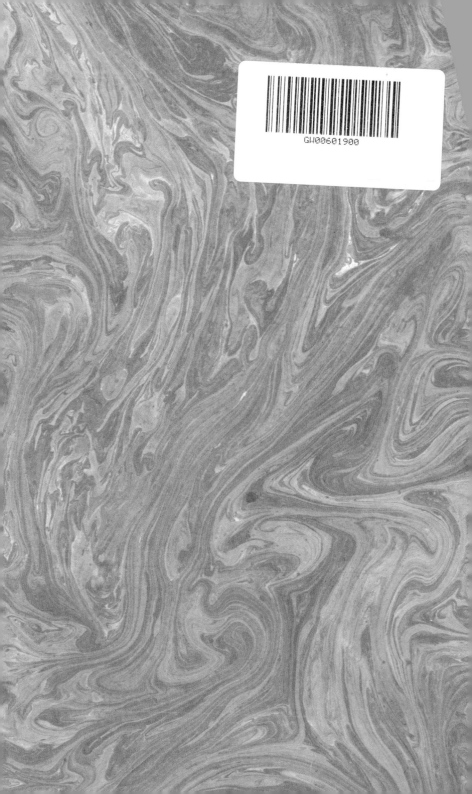

MYTHOLOGICAL GODS

MYTHOLOGICAL GODS

M. R. PADILLA

© EDIMAT BOOKS Ltd. London
is an affiliate of Edimat Libros S.A.
C/ Primavera, 35 Pol. Ind. El Malvar
Arganda del Rey - 28500 (Madrid) Spain
E-mail: edimat@edimat.es

Title: *Mythological Gods*
Author: *M. R. Padilla*

ISBN: 84-9794-025-3
Legal Deposit: M-48225-2004

PRINTED IN SPAIN

PROLOGUE

Who has not wondered at one time or another about the origins of the names of the planets, the stars and the constellations, or the names of the days of the week or the months?

And which of us has not asked ourselves about the great significance that Olympian gods had, or about the role of the mythical heroes such as Prometheus, the creator of the human race, or Medea, the great enchantress with hidden powers, or Pandora, the first woman bearer of Ossa, the origin of evil?

The answers to these and other enigmas can be found in the study of mythology. But what is mythology? Where did it come from, and why?

Practically everybody has heard of Pandora's Box, or Achilles' Heel. Or they at least sound familiar. Yet if we ask somebody what they know about mythology, the most likely answer is not very much. There are not many people who can explain the origin or evolution of mythology, or the relationship that it has with our modern-day culture.

We use expressions that are rooted in mythology all the time. Expressions such as 'the strength of Hercules' or 'the body of an Adonis'; we know how to recognise the constellations of Ursa Major and Cassiopeia; and we are familiar with the names of the planets and the signs of the zodiac. Even in our day to day life we find theatres called *The Apollo,* cars called *Pegasus*, the Italian telephone company that has Mercury as its symbol; and our children watch programmes on the television called *The Adventures of Ulysses in Space*. However, it is rarely that we stop and think about the distant origins of these names, or in their original meaning. The enormously rich legacy that we have received from ancient mythology forms a part of our culture today in so many common ways that we have forgotten the wonderful origins of the myths and legends.

As we will see, each society of the ancient world created its own gods. Myths and legends are a universal human invention. They have appeared in different eras and different places as explanations of the critical problems that the human race must always face, and which seem to be enigmas, such as earthquakes, cataclysms and seasonal changes. And this has given rise to the existence of Sumerian, Egyptian, Nordic, Indian, and Aztec mythology.

This book proposes to offer a collection of the enigmas of the most transcendent and inspiring mythology: that of the Greeks and the Romans, and this volume centres on the gods and their legends. In a later book we will concentrate on the study of the myths and legends of heroes, demi-gods and mortals. This is no exhaustive study, but an approach to 101 enigmas of classic mythology. We will give descriptions of the gods and goddesses and their legends, and analyses of their roles and significance where possible. In the last pages of the book there is a series of valuable annotations for the study and understanding of the exciting world of mythology.

I

INTRODUCTION TO MYTHOLOGY

All men need the gods.

Homer

1. WHAT IS MYTHOLOGY?

The word mythology comes form the Greek *mythos* which means fable, and *logos,* which means speech. The definition that we find in any dictionary will say that mythology is the collection of related myths and legends that constitute the traditional religion of a determined people. In the same way we can define a myth as the symbolic explanation of a fact through a story which is generally based on elements of fantasy. Aside from the myths, mythology is also full of legends, which are tales of uncertain events that have left no evidence, and which are traditionally presented as true history. Though they may deal with implausible events – or even magical ones, they are based around what is believed to be the truth. These myths and legends describe, for example, the history of inventions (Talus and the saw), and of the first harvests (Triptolemus and Demeter for wheat, or Dionysus for wine), or tell of the first discoveries, and give interesting and attractive explanations of all natural phenomena (the sun, the moon and the rainbow), and the origins of the first cities (Delphi and Rhodes).

Mythology at a first glance can seem cruel and immoral: parents who devour their sons, incestuous relationships between brothers and sisters or mothers and sons, and the like. But we must examine these tales from the point of view of an ancient society, in which the difference between the good and the bad, and the moral and the immoral was yet to be established.

With an unequalled beauty and richness, mythology was the first religion of the ancient societies, appearing in Greece in the year 3000 BC and surviving as late as 600 BC, which saw the birth of philosophy and labelled the believers of mythology as naïve and ignorant. But until then mythology was a source of seduction and originality within the ancient religions, enriching cultism and granting an element of terror to the sacred.

When referring to Ancient Greece, one should speak of religiousness rather than religion. Of a feeling of a relationship with the divinity that is implicit in everything. Unlike other religions, there was no dogmatic form, nor catechisms, nor preaching, nor even clergy, only excepting the oracles of the sanctuaries. Religion was passed by word of mouth from parents to children, through a wide variety of myths and legends, until in the year 800 BC the poet Homer, who is believed to have been blind, wrote *The Iliad* in which he tells the tale of Helen and the Trojan War, and *The Odyssey*, the account of the voyage of Ulysses. After Homer there was Hesiod, and from then on countless more until Pausianas at the end of the second century.

Greek mythology is not only a source of Greek religion, but also of universal and topical ideas that are still alive today, from which ancient peoples knew how best to reap benefits, and which still enriches our modern society today. Mythology stays alive because it remains close to human thought. Greek beliefs not only humanised the gods by giving them anthropomorphic forms, but it also personalised them with good and bad qualities.

The gods were not faithful husbands or submissive wives, neither were they obedient children, loving parents, chaste maidens or noble warriors. These gods were certainly not perfect, as could be first imagined, and they were represented as lustful, cruel and heartless. But as they are gods, they are blessed with superhuman strength and powers, and possess the gift of immortality, which, far from highlighting their difference from the world of mortals, values them as exemplary figures to whom humans could continuously relate, in addition to giving them respect and veneration.

On the other hand, mythology offers a multicoloured scene of mythical beings: Cyclops, Titans, hundred-armed monsters, nymphs, sirens, satyrs, centaurs, to name but a few, who share this magic world with the gods, demi-gods, heroes and humans, and who interrelate on frequent occasions and sometimes even maintain more intimate relations.

As we have already seen, the gods were of human form, although it is true that they were blessed with perfect physique, according to the Greek canon of beauty. But they also demonstrated generally human behaviour. This meant that they were characterised by human virtues and defects, such as loyalty, envy, generosity, jealousy, fidelity, ambition, and anger, in which we can all see reflections of ourselves. On the other hand, mythology abounds with myths and legends that tell us of the voyages of heroes whose moral and physical sufferings, whose doubts and worries concerning death, love, pain and the terror of fate, move us to sympathy.

But the Greeks were not satisfied with the simple humanisation of their gods; they went further, to the point of mixing their own world with the divine. Zeus, for example, had several adventures with mortals. Sometimes he had to confront them, such as in the myth of Prometheus and the Stolen Fire; or sometimes just to maintain his free will, as Homer reveals by making Athena say to Achilles: "I descend from the sky to mitigate your anger, if you will heed me."

For me, personally, mythology is an open manifestation of imagination, invented by ancient societies to give a poetic and exquisite but logical explanation of the enigmas contained within the surrounding world. Not in vain has the myth been considered as the first attempt at a comprehension of reality; an attempt to justify the world and the human race by going in search of a genesis.

Although there are important coinciding points between the different representations of the heavenly lands that rule the world and the conflicts between humans, each society developed its own system of beliefs through certain particular characteristics, which can only be approximately related.

As we will see, mythology is a changing and complex phenomenon, which is neither immobile nor static.

2. WHY WAS MYTHOLOGY BORN?

The answer to this enigma may seem simple, but it is actually very complex. There are numerous theories that have been established to determine the origin, function and significance of myths, especially since the 19th century. In addition, these studies have been undertaken within different spectrums of knowledge, and for that reason their direction depends on the field from which the theories of the origins of mythology are formed: philology, anthropology, philosophy, mythology or history.

The most generally accepted opinion among studies of today is that we cannot generalise one focus as the only one valid, but that all the different aspects must be simultaneously taken into consideration.

History shows us that our race has always, through any era, asked questions concerning the origins of the world, the human role in life, and death. There is not one culture or society, however small, that is known to have lacked an interest in who human beings are or where the world comes from. Through the times, the human race has found different answers to each of these enigmas.

Today, science has provided us with the answer to many of these enigmas, but until the discovery and investigations into science humans could only depend on one thing: their own imagination.

We know that humans, since their primitive origins, have contemplated the world around them: the sky, the Earth, water and the animals, and they have been surprised by what they have seen. If our race had been satisfied with accepting nature and the facts of life simply for what they are, things would probably have remained as they were, but fortunately humans are curious by nature, and once having satisfied their hunger, thirst and need for warmth, they were driven to look for a better understanding of their world. They needed to know everything, from why the seasons change, what force moves the ocean and creates the waves, or what paints a seven-coloured arch across the sky, to more profound questions such as what has created the human race and where do we go when we die.

For explanations of the origins of the human race and the world, every society in each different civilisation has searched for answers in religion; thus creating gods, beings far superior and more powerful than ourselves, who they could worship and even fear, and who bore the responsibility for everything that happened in the world, be it good or bad: cataclysms, beneficial rain, earthquakes or abundant harvests.

For these reasons, before the appearance of Christianity in Norway, people believed that Thor travelled through the sky in a carriage pulled by two Billy goats, beating his powerful hammer to create thunder and lightning. The Norwegian word for thunder *torden* means literally 'noise of Thor'. Normally when there is thunder and lightning there is also rain, and rain was vital for Viking farmers, so Thor was worshipped as the god of fertility. In other words, the mythical explanation for rain was that Thor banged his hammer to make the rain fall and nourish the ground.

All the other ancient civilisations also created their own mythical systems, by using an imaginative concept of the world to express and explain the origins of things, the phases of existence, atmospheric phenomena, and much more. In this way the different mythologies were developed: the Sumerian, Egyptian, Nordic, Hindu, and Greek.

Here lies the explanation for why the myths of each society are similar: they were created to fulfil the same needs. In fact societies have also borrowed myths and legends from each other and then adapted them to their particular idiosyncrasy. This has led at times to the appearance of gods whose origins are difficult to trace, or of confusion between two very similar myths.

We can say that the human race began to emerge from the mists of ignorance and irrationality towards the light of thought and consciousness. In this true birth of the race as an intelligent being there were various stages, amongst which mythology, together with religious magic and ritual, occupies a fundamental position.

Theories on the origin of mythology

Various theories have been suggested to explain the origins of *myths*:

a) According to the allegories of the Ionic philosophers, the gods were the personification of the elements, physical forces such as air, sun, water, thunder, etc, or of moral concepts.

b) In the fourth century BC, the Greek philosopher Evemero claimed that myths were no more than the idealised records about mortal kings and heroes, written after their death. His disciples later took his theories further, declaring for example, that Zeus was a king of Crete and his war with the Titans no more than an attempt to repress an uprising; or that Atlas was an astronomer, who for this reason only was said to bear the weight of the world on his shoulders.

c) This theory was adopted and accepted by the Church during the Middle Ages, as it provided an easy interpretation of Paganism.

d) Modern revelations of Oriental, American, African, and Oceanic mythology complicated the problem and created a comparative mythology in an attempt to classify and explain the origin of all the beliefs. The aim was to explain them all through common tradition, originating in the Orient and according to the psychological condition of primitive humans, who tended to trust only what they could sense physically and who believed that anything with its own

12

Zeus.

movement or force, like the sun and the elements, was an analogous life form (anthropomorphism). As these primitive peoples migrated, they carried their beliefs with them, which explains the diffusion and modification of mythology in relation to other cults.

e) In the seventeenth century, philosophers came to the conclusion that the bible was the pure form of history, and mythology was a distorted version of the original revelation.

f) In the nineteenth century, philosophers tried to demonstrate that mythology was born from the deformation of language, in the same way that a pearl is created from the deformity of an oyster. Meanwhile, anthropologists, basing their theories on studies of comparative mythology, declared that "it is humans and human thought, blended with human language, that naturally and necessarily created the strange conglomeration of the ancient fable".

Philosophers now believe that all myths were originally myths about nature, separated into different categories such as the sun, the sky, the moon, or the sea, in addition to those about the Underworld and the demons that inhabited its dark regions. The Greeks have forgotten that Zeus used to mean 'bright sky', just as the word 'ostracism' has lost all connection with the shell of the oyster. In this way, we can see how the meanings of myths have been lost alongside the loss of the original meaning of language. Such anomalies in mythology, together with the entanglement of individual myths, has resulted in it being impossible to disentangle the original significance of each one, much like a ball of snow that rolls down the mountainside picking up dirt, rocks, and plants along with the snow and ends up as an agglomeration of analogous, foreign elements that hide the original nucleus from view.

The reality that several myths may exist to explain one phenomenon can be clarified by the fact that each situation is altered by circumstance, resulting in the mythological roles of the sun or rain, for example, which can be beneficial in some cases and disastrous in others. Thus, the Sun god can be represented as both a good and fertile god and a cruel and vengeful force, depending on the story.

3. GREEK MYTHOLOGY

As we have seen over the millennia and throughout the world, an extensive range of mythological explanations has formed in answer to philosophical questions. From amongst all these various mythological histories, that of Ancient Greece glows with its own splendour. Therefore, we dedicate this volume to the study of Greek mythology and the Roman mythology that evolved from it.

Not without reason, Bruno Snell affirmed: "European thought began with the Ancient Greeks, and there has been no other form of thought since then". The existentialist philosopher Jaspers also claimed that "philosophy was born in Greece, because that is where humans were amazed by reality, and that amazement brought questions and doubts". Many years before philosophy, mythology was invented – more prolific, emblematic, and enigmatic, and which has been the inspiration for writers and artists throughout the ages, extending its domain to include the whole world.

Until around the seventh century BC, when philosophy first took hold in Greece, mythology was responsible for providing the answers to philosophical questions, and these explanations were transmitted from generation to generation. It could be said that the human view of the world until that point was mythical.

Though the first myths and legends in Greece were adapted from older traditions, this heritage was soon overtaken by its own mythology. A good example of this creative borrowing is the story of the tasks of Heracles (Hercules in Roman form). The recent discovery of an epic summary of the similar tasks of 'Ninurta', son of the god of the Air, Enlil, eradicates all traces of doubt.

Greek civilisation and its extraordinary mythology were based around three principal elements: topography, the unique way of life, and the language.

a) *Topography*. Greece's geographic location obliged its people to become sailors, as it is the Mediterranean country with the most coastline. The topography of the country was the source of many myths related to primitive settlings.

Almost all the tales name places like Sparta, Delphi, Mycenae, Troy, Athens, or Thebes. The Indo-Europeans and their religion and gods arrived via Mount Olympus, Greece's highest summit at 9,573 feet, located between Macedonia and Thessaly. Popular imagination took this fact, together with the height and inaccessibility of the mountain's misty peaks, and attributed the place to the gods, calling them Olympians.

b) *The way of life*. This played a very significant part in the origins and evolution of mythology. The rich and cultured members of Greek society enjoyed a large amount of free time, as they had slaves to carry out all their work. They therefore devoted themselves to recreation and mental pursuits. Meetings were held in the public squares to think, put forward ideas, and form discussions. Greek society could be said to be the most erudite, refined and sybaritic culture of all times.

c) *The language*. The subtlety and diversity of Ancient Greek founded speculation about the nature of existence. In the ninth century BC, poets like Homer entertained the people with exciting tales, such as the Trojan War.

This is not the most opportune moment to offer a more general exposition of Greek evolution, from agrarian culture through a process of anthropomorphism to the democratisation of the Dionysian cults. But we should emphasise its cohesive significance within the city, in the cult of the votive gods, and on a national scale as a seed of national relations, in the cults of the great sanctuaries such as Olympus, Delphi, or Eleusis.

4. ROMAN MYTHOLOGY

When the Republic of Rome was proclaimed in 509 BC, the Greek world was already culturally and artistically advanced. The Romans had not yet defined their identity as a society, at least the identity that they were to achieve as the Roman Empire. This alone is enough to explain Roman mythology's dependence on its Greek counterpart, just as its art was dependent on Greek art. But Greece was not the only source for Roman mythology. The influences that affected the Roman people until the beginnings of the Empire can be summarised in the following elements:

Primitive Italic cultures: The Etruscan culture, which was a decisive factor in determining several of the singular characters of Roman society, introducing, for example, the Cult of the Dead. The Etruscans had previously established a society in the region of Etruria or Tuscany, but although the origins of this people were always thought to be in Asia Minor, today it is believed that they may have originated in Etruria itself.

Greek culture: When the Romans conquered Greece, an authentic cultural colonisation of the conquerors by the defeated people occurred. Not only did the conquerors absorb Greek mythology, they also took hundreds of artists as slaves, as well as shipments of sculptures and even architectonic elements. It should be pointed out that Roman citizens did not feel their 'nationality' in the same way as we would understand it today; the Roman was a citizen of the capital city by denomination only and felt 'Roman' according to individual associations with the centre of the Empire. No other Empire in history has been named after its capital city, and this does not give the image of a Roman people humiliated by a lack of art in their society, in comparison with the Greeks' accomplishments, nor a people who were ashamed to adopt the gods of their conquered cultures into their own.

However, it would be a great error to believe that Roman mythology was a crude imitation of the Greek, or even a simple extension of it, as the Roman citizen is by no means an imitation of the Greek citizen. The Romans believed that their essential mission was to govern and control the extensive world under their rule. The Greek citizen attended the meetings on the square to resolve the vital questions of existence, but the family did not feature as an important element in Greek social structure as it did in Rome, where it was a fundamental aspect of society.

17

Greek mythology and legend were of great interest to the Romans, who had never given their gods human form, nor had any intertwining network of mythology relating to them. Gradually their king of the gods, Jupiter, came to be considered as Zeus, the Greek counterpart, and other gods and goddesses were also combined. The definitive fusion between Greek and Roman worship came about in 148 BC, after the Romans had occupied the entire Greek land.

With Greece's decadence in the second century and the growing predominance of Rome, Greek mythology became completely Latinized. The Romans continued to worship their local gods by their original names, but the more powerful gods were assimilated to the Greek deities.

But Rome was not influenced by Greece alone. Both societies were affected by outside influences. As both cultures extended their dominion across the shores of the Mediterranean, their pantheon acquired an increasing number of foreign gods. Some simply were assimilated into the culture, as in the case of Anubis, the Egyptian god who ended up with the characteristics and attributions of Hermes; or Dusares, the sun god of the Arabs, who came to be confused with Dionysus.

There were also divinities, on the other hand, who gave additional identity to an Olympian god, such as Doliqueno, the Asian god whose name is sometimes used in place of Jupiter. We also know of gods such as Horus or the goddess Atargatis, who adopted other names as they were absorbed into the divine Greek and Roman circles, the former becoming Harpocrates and the latter Dea Syria.

Occasionally, the Romans worshipped a foreign god by his original name, such as in the cases of Mithra and Elagabal. However, despite these numerous assimilations and transformations, the Roman people always maintained respect for foreign gods, never using religion or political convictions as a reason to strip them of their primitive attributions. They understood that adopting the gods of their conquered lands was a way of ensuring the loyalty of the subjects to the all-powerful empire.

5. COMMON THEMES OF MYTHOLOGY

There is a series of elements repeated through the different myths and legends of which we should be aware. However, these elements are not present in any systematic or isolated form, and two or three may appear in one legend and one in another:

a) *Immortality*. This was generally granted to all the gods, who fed on nectar and ambrosia. On occasion, mortals were given the gift, such as the fisherman Glaucus, who ate a magic herb and was transformed into a god of the sea. There also exist cases where immortality was exchanged for death: Chiron the centaur preferred the tranquillity of death to eternal suffering and gave his immortality to Prometheus.

b) *Transformation and metamorphosis*. Metamorphosis was a sign of the presence of the gods and appears in mythology as the essential development or the conclusion to the legend. All sorts of metamorphosis were normal: animal, vegetable, and even mineral, in order to escape the amorous advances of the gods or humans, or the fury of an enemy; the gods were also able to transform themselves with the aim of seducing or overcoming their lovers. Though on other occasions, such transformations were due to the brutal and irredeemable rage of divine punishments, when the victims were transformed into statues and condemned to eternal immobility. Metamorphosis could also be a gift from a god, in reward for a good deed, as in the tale of Philemon and Baucis, transformed into trees in return for their hospitality to Zeus and Hermes.

Without a doubt, for humans, the ability to transform one's form and essence is the highest demonstration of divine power. Whereas immortality can go unappreciated by humans, metamorphosis is a power that is both visible and tangible.

c) *Usurpation of the position of parents or elders*. This can be a real usurpation, in the case of Cronus or Zeus, or simply a feared usurpation, and often predicted by an oracle, as in the case of Oedipus.

d) *Death or attempted murder of a son or daughter*. The

19

clearest example is that of Cronus devouring his children.

e) *Revenge*. Killing or seducing an enemy's wife, or killing his children. Also included in this category is the son or daughter who avenges or protects the parents, and the jealous wife who avenges herself on an unfaithful husband.

f) *Fire*. A very significant feature, this also symbolises giving or recovery of something. The fire that gives immortality, so necessary for sacrifices, is also a divine cathartic or purifying element.

g) *Punishment of impiety*. For a mortal who attempts to marry a god, such as the tale of Ixion and Hera; or when a human tries to beat a god, always seen as insolent, and always punished with an everlasting penalty, as for Prometheus.

h) *The presence of giants, monsters, serpents etc.*, which can have either of two meanings, one of which is good, as the guardian of a treasure, such as Ladon, the guardian dragon of the golden apples; and one which is bad, such as the destructive creatures that must be killed. Many of these monsters have forms that are half-human and half-animal, such as the sphinx, the sirens, and the Minotaur.

i) *Disputes amongst members of a family*. This is the price of ambition and greed. The example of fighting between brothers can be seen in the war of the Titans.

j) *The founding of cities*, according to an oracle, following an animal or instructions, or simply fleeing from a punishment.

k) *Special weapons* and methods of defence necessary for the destruction of an enemy, as in the case of Hades, who becomes invisible, or Zeus' powerful lightning.

l) *Extraordinary or unusual births*. Prometheus forges a man from clay, which bears a faint relation to the origins of humans in Christian legend. Other examples are the birth of Aphrodite from the semen of Uranus, or that of Athena who is born from Zeus' head.

m) *Mortal lovers* of the gods.

n) *Incestuous relationships* between members of the same family.

However, these last two points, as well as others related to sex, need a chapter of their own.

Hermes, Orpheus and Euripides.

6. SEX AND MYTHOLOGY

The Greeks did not have the same understanding of sexology as we have today. Greeks were an uninhibited people that readily accepted promiscuity and homosexuality, and the gods' sexual behaviour may sometimes seem unusual and unacceptable to modern people. Zeus was the king of sexual insatiability, and his behaviour may not seem like the exemplary model we expect from a divine being. However, we must read such occurrences in context and bear in mind the social and cultural values of the people who created these myths, who we know had a different moral outlook from the one we may have today. We also must avoid falling into the trap of believing that mythology is a mere transposition of Greek customs, as the gods were also seen as polygamous, incestuous, or immoral by Greek society, which was not accustomed to behave according to the same principles.

The explanation of the origins of the world and the profound interrelations between different human activities required their creators or divine representatives to be able to reproduce and marry amongst themselves without excessive prejudice. Zeus, for example, believed the duty of paternity was more important than being faithful to Hera, as it meant the expansion of his reign over the worlds of the gods and humans. Neither must we forget that, in mythology, much of this behaviour carries implicit punishment. Hera, the faithful wife of Zeus who does not understand her husband's reasoning, punishes his lovers mercilessly.

Sex was so important to Greek mythology that its influence may be proven easily. We only have to observe the legacy left to us in our sexual lexis that is intimately related to *Aphrodite*, with her Roman name *Venus* and her assistant *Eros*. In our vocabulary we have the words '*aphrodisiac*', to define something that stimulates the sexual appetite; '*erotic*', and all its derivations, to describe sexual connotations; and '*venereal*', used to describe sexually transmitted disease.

Further lexical heritage can be seen in the word '*hermaphrodite*', meaning a being of both sexes. The word is derived from Hermes and Aphrodite, who had a son they called *Hermaphrodite*. Legend tells us that he grew to become a youth of exceptional beauty. While he was travelling through Asia Minor, he bathed one day in the waters of the Salmacis Stream, where a beautiful nymph lived. The nymph was struck by the good-looking youth and fell in love with him, but Hermaphrodite was uninterested. So the nymph threw herself on the young man, wrapping herself around him, and begged the gods to keep them united forever. The gods granted her desire by combining their bodies to form a single being of both sexes.

The myth of *Androgena*, similar to that of Hermaphrodite, is told in Plato's *The Banquet*. According to the philosopher, the mortal was of both sexes, but the gods were fearful of such power and divided the being into two, thus creating men and women.

Aphrodite, the origin of all that relates to love and erotic desire, was also united with Dionysus, the god of the orgies that followed his drunken worshipping, and Pryapus was born from the union, a being blessed with a sexual organ of enormous proportions and continually erect, who was unable to copulate and, thus, created *masturbation*. His cult was located in a region on the shores of the Hellespont, the same place where Aphrodite abandoned her son, fearful of being made to look ridiculous for having given birth to a deformed child. In time, the cult extended throughout Italy, where it was very popular, and Pryapus became a fertility god, both for his emblem of the great erect phallus and for his parents. He ensured the breeding of livestock, the birth of bees, and the production of the vineyards. People put a phallic stone in their private gardens and orchards to encourage flowers and fruit.

Lastly, the word '*hymen*', which denominates the membrane that partially covers the vagina on virgins, is named after Hymen, another son of Aphrodite and Dionysus, or of Apollo and a muse, according to some legends. In the ancient world, Hymen was the god of marriage, who presided and personified the nuptial hymns. Various legends have been created to justify his invocation in the course of the wedding ceremony. However, they all tell that his beauty rivalled even that of Apollo, for which reason he was later attributed the very emblems of matrimony by artists: the nuptial torch, the flute, and the crown of roses. Hymen means marriage: the bond of Hymen.

As we have seen, the Ancients were not polygamists, but the gods were permitted to act freely upon their desires. Therefore there are many legends about Zeus' extramarital affairs and the amorous adventures of Aphrodite and Apollo, who let themselves be led by their passions. It should be noted that the impunity of the gods in this sense meant that they forced women, both mortal and immortal, to satisfy their sexual needs, without receiving any punishment for this violation. Seen in this way, mythology is rife with *rape*. The only woman that Zeus did not abuse by raping her was Alcmene, whom he seduced by wooing her disguised as her husband Amphytrion.

But in comparison to all this promiscuous behaviour, we have Hera, the perfectly faithful wife, and the virgin goddesses, also called the *vestal goddesses*. Simply seeing them naked constituted a heinous sin, avenged by a horrible death. The three goddesses that symbolised purity were Hestia, the goddess of fire; Athena, of intelligence; and Artemis, of nature. The first was Greek, or Indo-European; the second Mediterranean or Cretan; and the third Asian.

A common point in the amorous adventures of almost all the gods is that of metamorphosis or transformation into plants, animals, and other forms. Zeus had a great ability for transforming himself into different figures in order to take lovers: he was a bolt of lightning, a golden rain, an eagle, a bull, a serpent, and a swan. It is not easy to describe the erotic charms or the sexuality of an animal, as this is classed as *zoophilia*, sex between a human and an animal. It is supposed that Eros obliged Zeus to transform himself into different animals, to fool the jealous Hera and obtain his lovers.

From metamorphosis we continue to another form of transformation: *transvestism*, which is given its clearest example by Dionysus, who was dressed as a girl to escape the clutches of Hera when he was just a few months old. He later appeared before the three daughters of Minia disguised as a girl.

24

Within the subject of sex in mythology, *incest* is perhaps the most controversial. Humans are horrified at the behaviour of some gods who commit incest with no sign of guilt or shame, including Gaea and her relationships with Pontus and Uranus; Cronus and his sister Rhea; and Zeus, who has sexual relations with his sisters Hera and Demeter.

Lastly, *homosexuality* is also very open in the world of the gods. Zeus was known to have only one amorous adventure with a man. The legend, from Asia Minor, tells that Zeus fell in love with the handsome Ganymede, the son of Tros and Calirrhoe, and turning himself into an eagle, he caught him in his talons and carried him off to Olympus. Once there he replaced Hebe as his personal wine pourer.

But the most beautiful legend of homosexuality tells of Hyacinth, a youth whose favours were argued over by several gods, including Apollo. It is said that Zephyr, jealous of Apollo's affection for Hyacinth, blew a stone that Apollo had thrown in a game of hopscotch with Hyacinth and made it hit the young man on the forehead. In response to the action, and to perpetuate his love for Hyacinth, Apollo turned the blood flowing from the wound into a purple flower in the form of an iris, whose petals bear the Greek word 'ay', which means 'what a disgrace!', as well as being the Greek initial for Hyacinth, '?'.

7. HOW HAS MYTHOLOGY INFLUENCED WORLD CULTURE?

In mythology, we find the components that have modelled the history of our Western humanistic culture. In a certain way, Greco-Roman mythology is the origin of subjects that later became literature, morals, human societies, and, on occasion, science. Ancient Greek culture, particularly, created a wide-ranging mythology whose influence in philosophy and the arts is still strong today.

Art.–The works of sculpture inspired by mythology are countless: Praxiteles' *Hermes with the young Dionysus*, the *Venus de Milo*, Cellini's *Perseus with the head of Medusa*;

as are paintings: Veronese's *Rape of Europa*, Titian's *Venus and Adonis*, and Botticelli's *The Birth of Venus*. Magnificent temples and sanctuaries have been erected in their honour, such as the splendid temple of Artemis in Ephesus, and the impressive temple of Zeus, as well as innumerable bas-reliefs, ceramics, tapestries, etc.

Humanities.–Mythology has not only had a huge influence on the visual arts, but also on literature, astronomy, and culture in general. References to classic mythology abound in diverse forms throughout each artistic era. The perfect literary example is one of the most important contemporary literary works: *Ulysses* by Irish writer James Joyce (1882–1941), who, inspired by Plato's Greek hero in *The Iliad*, wrote epic about a day in the life of a twentieth-century Irishman. *Apollo*, the Greek god of beauty, has lent his name to numerous theatres and cultural and artistic centres. Mythology is the mother of Greek theatre, where each performance began with the religious rites in honour of Dionysus. The first theatrical works were written by Thespis in around 540–534; and the clearest portrayers of tragedy were Aeschylus and Sophocles, just as Aristophanes was for comedy.

Astronomy.–When we look at the sky and try to distinguish the stars and planets, the names we use are mostly those of mythological gods and goddesses. Many constellations, planets, and even satellites were given the names of classic ancient deities, according to the particular characteristics perceived in them, and whose attributes and histories were, at the same time, an imaginary transposition from the origins of the universe.

In this way, for example, the tiny planet Mercury, the closest to the sun, received the Roman name of the Greek god Hermes, the messenger of the gods. Its mythological name is quite apt if we think of how swiftly the wing-footed god could fly, making it difficult for humans to see him in the sky, much like the planet *Mercury*, which can be seen only immediately after sunset and before sunrise. *Venus*, known by the Greeks since the sixth century BC, has been named the twilight star of dawn and dusk. Its brilliance reigns in the sky during the hours of twilight in honour of

Venus.

the Roman version of the Greek goddess of love – Aphrodite of Near East – born from the spray of the sea. *Mars*, the Greek counterpart of Ares, was separated from his lover Venus by the Earth, and like both of them, Mars is a rocky planet of a similar size and relatively close to the sun. While the high temperature on Venus excludes the possibility of a manned expedition, Mars offers a hospitable atmosphere. There will be a strong symbolical significance when the old god of war, with his accompanying satellites *Phobos* and *Deimos*, his sons (discovered in 1877 by A. Hall), renounces his anger and allows humans to conquer his terrain. However, we should remember that the scenes Hephaestus worked into the shield of Homer's Achilles ironically were pastoral images of peace and prosperity. Mars was named *Pyroente* (fire bearer).

With sixteen natural satellites orbiting a planet that is two-and-a-half times bigger than any other in the known solar system, Jupiter is the giant that honours the name of the king of the gods, the Roman counterpart of Zeus, the father of the Olympian gods. *Saturn*, the Roman version of Cronus, is the second-largest planet and has the lowest density in the solar system. More spectacular than terrible, with the distinctive rings that circle the planet, it is suited to its mythological character of the god who was defeated and dethroned by his son. Another giant, still four times larger than the Earth, is old *Uranus*, composed of a thick gaseous blanket.

Neptune is the fourth giant of the solar system. Because of its size – and perhaps some other aspects still to be learned in detail – it is Uranus' twin. It is too far away to be seen with the naked eye and, in fact, was discovered due to the influence that its gravitational pull produces on the orbit of Uranus. Le Verrier gave the planet the Roman name of the Greek god Poseidon in 1846, according to astronomic tradition, just as W. Lassell called the satellite that he discovered in the same year *Triton*, and G. P. Kuiper named the planet's second satellite *Nereide* in 1949, in reference to Amphitrite.

As in the case of Neptune, the discovery of the far-away *Pluto* was possible due to a prediction. In reality, the god that presides over the Underworld, and who lends his name to this small, cold, and dark world, is as badly represented in the solar system as his sombre mythological significance in the culture of humans on the Earth.

There exists a legend to explain the *Milky Way*, the astral contour of the galaxy. According to its mythical origins, it was formed by drops of milk that were spilt when Hera took Heracles from her breast, for he sucked with such strength that he hurt her. A jet of milk shot out into the sky at great speed and became the *Milky Way*. Etymologically, 'galaxy' is the same as 'lacteal', or milk.

In addition to the planets, there are stars and constellations with mythological names, such as *the Hyades*, the daughters of Atlas, which means 'rains'. Their names were Ambrosia, Eudora, Coronis, Polyxo, Phaio, Dione, and Aisyle. Legend tells us that in mourning for the death of their brother Hiante in Libya, killed by a wild beast, they appealed to the supreme god. To console the sisters and stop their tears he turned them into stars, but they still did not stop weeping, hence the name Hyades. The stars' appearance coincides with the spring rains. Their sisters *the Pleiads*, Maia, Electra, Tayete, Asterope, Merope, Alcione, and Celaena, were converted into stars by Zeus when he saved them from persecution by Orion. Their appearance in May, during spring (in Latin they were called *Vergiliae*, meaning 'see the spring'), would indicate to sailors that the weather would be fair ('pleiades' comes from an Ancient Greek word meaning 'to navigate'), and when they disappeared from view, at the beginning of September, it signalled the start of bad weather and danger for sailors.

Callisto, the daughter of Lycaon, was seduced by Zeus while he was disguised as Apollo, and Arcas was born from their union. To save her from the rage of Hera, he turned her into a bear and transported her to the stars, where she occupied a place amongst the constellations and was called *Ursa Major* – the Great Bear and *Ursa Minor* – the Little Bear. However, Poseidon, in answer to Hera's pleas, forbade him to put the constellation on the horizon.

Legends also exist about the constellations of *Cepheus, Cassiopeia, Amaltea, Auriga, Ariadne*, and *Orion*, amongst others. In the Northern Hemisphere, we find the constellations of Perseus, Andromeda, and Pegasus. *Perseus* has the form of a bell, through which pass shooting stars called the Perseids. In *Andromeda*, which appears in the form of a figure with folded arms, is the Star Cloud of Andromeda, the furthest celestial body from the Earth that can be seen with the naked eye. *Pegasus* can be distinguished from the four bright stars that form the Square of Pegasus.

Astrology.–The Zodiac is the celestial path on either side of the ecliptic, made up of twelve constellations, each symbolising a myth, a legend, or a figure:

ARIES, the ram, who in mythology wore the Golden Fleece.

TAURUS, the bull, the animal that kidnapped Europa.

GEMINI, the twins, which signify the Dioscuri twins: Polydeuces and Castor.

CANCER, the crab, which was the giant beast sent by Hera to bite Heracles.

LEO, the lion, killed by Heracles in Nemea.

VIRGO, the virgin, to some Astrea, the just and virtuous daughter of Zeus and Themis, who lived amongst mortals in the Golden Age. But when the human soul was corrupted, she left their world and fled to the sky, amongst the stars, where she received the name Virgo.

LIBRA, the scales, is the attribute of the goddess Justice.

SCORPIO, the scorpion, sent by Artemis to sting Orion.

SAGITTARIUS, the centaur, in the image of the wise centaur Chiron.

CAPRICORN, the goat, is the emblem of Zeus' wet-nurse, the goat Amaltea.

AQUARIUS, the water carrier, Ganymede.

PISCES, the fish, signifies the shoal of fish that carried Cupid and Aphrodite on their back to escape from Typhon.

The days of the week and the months.–Astralism is a variant of the allegory, which is based on the belief that myths come from the primitive worship of the Sun, the Moon, and the stars, and is simply a way of describing the existence, orbits, and other properties and appearances of the stars. Each day of the week, for example, has the name of the divine astral beings:

> SOLIS DIES > DOMINICA DIES (the day of the Lord or the Sun).
> LUNAE DIES (the Moon, or the goddess Semele or her Roman counterpart Diana).
> MARTIS DIES (the planet Mars, and the god Mars or Ares).
> MERCURII DIES (the planet Mercury, and the god Mercury or Hermes).
> JOVIS DIES (the planet Jupiter, and the god Jupiter or Zeus).
> VENERIS DIES (the planet Venus, and the goddess Venus or Aphrodite).
> SATURNI DIES > SABRATON DIES (the day of rest for the Lord, or the god Saturn).

Some languages change the first and the last days, especially Italian and French. The romance languages maintain these Latin roots, while in English common nomenclature is derived from the names of the corresponding Saxon gods. The Latin names are also used in legislative and judicial language.

The names of the months correspond to the following gods:

> JANUARIUS (January) from the two-headed Roman god *Janus*, who could see in opposite directions, one toward the year that we leave behind and the other toward the new year. He is related to the fortunes of war.

FEBRUARIUS (February) was the month dedicated to purification.

MARTIUS (March) the month of Mars, god of war. This was the month that soldiers returned to war. It is also the month that Juno conceived Mars.

APRILIS (April) the month of the goddess Venus.

MAIUS (May) the month of the goddess Maia, and the month of flowers and the goddess Flora.

JUNIUS (June) the month of the goddess Juno, or Hera.

Psychology.–This science, centred in the opposite field to mythology, has taken some of its starting points from legends, not only to denominate an atmospheric phenomenon, a star, or a part of the human body, but also to channel an interpretation of a determined human behavioural pattern. The myths of *Oedipus* or *Electra*, for example, have been used to denominate a type of behaviour. These usually correspond to emotional conflicts that are common in the early childhood stage of human development.

* * *

To conclude, I would like to emphasise a single thought, summarising some of the ideas we have explored so far: "Mythology is born from the imperious human need to justify and explain the enigmas of the world, and, to that end, they employ their imagination to create a series of myths and legends that have formed a part of world culture." Our imagination is prodigious, and mythology is a fine demonstration of that.

II

THE BIRTH OF THE GODS

In the beginning there was Chaos.

Hesiod

1. FROM CHAOS CAME THE FIRST GODS

In the beginning, there existed nothing more than a confused and formless mass over which *Chaos* ruled, sharing his throne with his queen *Nyx* or Nox, the dark goddess of night. In the eternity of their kingdom, the two deities decided to seek the help of their son *Erebus*, which means 'darkness'. The first thing he decided to do was dethrone his father and unite himself with his mother, with whom he had two children: *Aether* (light) and *Hemera* (day), who dethroned both their parents, in time, and transformed the chaotic world into a beautiful kingdom with the help of their son, *Eros* (love). They also produced other children, *Gaea* (earth) and *Pontus* (sea).

In this way, Eros embellished Gaea with exuberant nature, beautiful and wild, and she responded by creating *Uranus* (sky). So it was that these last two were more powerful than their predecessors, and they exiled them and ruled in their place.

Some time later, Gaea and Uranus produced an extensive dynasty: twelve TITANS (six males and six females): *Oceanus, Coeus, Crius, Hyperion, Iapetus, Cronus, Theia, Rhea, Tethys, Themis, Mnemosyne* and *Phoebe*. The Titans were giant beings, so powerful that Uranus detested them, as he believed he would follow the fate of his parents. In order to prevent this, he threw each of his children, soon after their births, into a deep, dark abyss, called *Tartarus*.

After the twelve Titans, Gaea and Uranus engendered three CYCLOPS: *Brontes* (thunder), *Steropes* (lightning) and *Arges* (sheet lightning), and three HECATONCHEIRES, or hundred-hands: *Cottus, Briareus,* and *Gyes*. The Cyclops were fantastic beings with a single eye in the centre of their forehead, and the Hecatoncheires were giants with a hundred arms and fifty heads. They were all thrown into Tartarus with their brothers and sisters.

But Gaea was not in agreement with Uranus. She was angry at his treatment of their children and swore vengeance. She descended into Tartarus and urged the Titans, the more intelligent of her offspring, to conspire against their father and dethrone him. The Titans were suspicious, and none save Cronus, the youngest and most daring, were bold enough to follow his mother's instructions. So Cronus took the scythe, the symbol of death, that his mother gave him, and taking Uranus by surprise while he slept, castrated him, holding his genitals with his left hand, which since then is considered the hand of ill-omen. He chopped them off and then threw them along with the scythe into Cape Drepanum. But he spilt three drops of blood, which fell onto Mother Earth and became the three Furies, or *Erinyes*, who avenge crimes of parricide and perjury. Enraged at such abuse, Uranus cursed Cronus, and prophesised that he would also one day be dethroned by his own son.

Cronus decided to free only the Titans from Tartarus, and he married his sister Rhea. In an impartial act, he decided to share the governing of the world with his brothers and sisters, giving Oceanus the reign of the great masses of water, which then took his name; to Tethys he gave the rivers; to Hyperion the sun; and to Phoebe the moon (both stars were believed to be transported by carts).

In the days of prosperity on Earth, the Titans inter-married. Oceanus married Tethys, and they had some three thousand *Oceanids*, including the famous *Eurynome, Metis, Dione,* and *Clymene*. Clymene then married Iapetus and bore *Atlas, Menoetius, Prometheus,* and *Epimetheus,* who later became prominent figures of Greek mythology. Hyperion and Theia produced *Helios*, the Sun, *Selene*, the Moon, and *Eos*, the Dawn.

The peace of this kingdom was broken with the arrival of the descendants of the supreme god. Cronus, fearful of his father's prediction, decided to finish with them. He ate them whole as soon as they were born, before the horror and helplessness of Rhea, whose pleas and weeping did nothing to change his mind.

When Rhea became pregnant for the sixth time, she decided that the moment had arrived to act, and so she resolved to trick her brother and husband. When he asked her to hand over the new-born child, she slyly wrapped a stone in the baby's blankets and gave them to him. Cronus devoured quickly, not even looking at the bundle, and went away satisfied. Then Rhea, who knew that she could not bring the child up without Cronus finding out, entrusted the care of the baby, called Zeus, to the *Melian Nymphs*, Adrastea and Io, who hid him in a cave on Mount Ida. There he was brought up with Pan, who became his adoptive brother, and both were nurtured by the goat *Amaltea*, who was later rewarded with a place in the sky as a constellation.

So that the cries of the baby were not heard by Cronus, the *Curetes*, or Korubantes, who were Rhea's priestesses, beat their weapons and danced, giving penetrating screams and chanting songs of battle, drowning out the noise of the infant. Zeus reached puberty amongst the shepherds of Ida, and the day came when Zeus fulfilled the prophecy, and, aided by Rhea and Metis, Oceanus' daughter, he surprised his father in an attack that defeated him. Then he forced him to drink a potion to make him vomit, concocted by Metis, which made Cronus first vomit the stone and then all his devoured children, one by one: Poseidon, Hades, Hestia, Demeter, and Hera.

Zeus divided the reign of the world between his siblings, as his father had done, and installed them on Mount Olympus, the highest mountain he could find. But only the wisest Titans – Mnemosyne, Themis, Oceanus and Hyperion, submitted to the new rule. The others named Atlas, son of Iapetus, as the chief of the Titans that stood against Zeus, as Cronus' strength was beginning to fade. So started the first war of history, a civil war that saw siblings fighting against each other.

Analysis and comments

In his work *Theogony* (116–113 BC), Hesiod considers chaos to be a matrix of the universe and resolves that the seeds of opposition manifested in the world must be attributed to it. The contrasts of the permanent tension between light and shadow, life and death, spiritual and material, and so on, all emerge from chaos.

As we can observe, the creating force of the universe was not an intelligent and personal being, which lived eternally and created the world with its own will from nothing, but rather a primal material in which the different beings gradually developed their form: gods, humans, and animals. Once the chaos became organised, it was called the Cosmos, which means 'order, world, universe'. The theory of the universe's formation is called Cosmogony.

Thus, cosmogony is the birth of order in the world, the organisation of places, time, the cycle of the seasons, the movement of the stars, and the sacred beings. Cosmogony implies theogony, which is the birth of the gods, and for this reason it is important to know the order in which they were born, how they procreate so as not to create hatred between them, and how to worship them. It also includes the organisation of language, just as, in the Bible, Adam gave names to all living things. This is the social order, the role of humans under a god or a divine being.

The Hecatoncheires and the Cyclops are the personifications of the material forces of nature, which always place obstacles and difficulties in the path of the definitive development of the constant and ordered ways of life. They correspond to the first phase of world organisation, preparing it to receive the different species from the animal and plant kingdoms.

Uranus, father and brother of these forces, rebels against them and throws them into Tartarus; Gaea, in turn, rebels against her husband and frees her children. This could be interpreted as Mother Nature freeing the natural phenomena to manifest themselves and follow their natural course.

Cronus rebels against Uranus for repeatedly making Gaea pregnant and the devastation of the Earth with his violence against his other children. He castrates his father, who cannot die because he is a god; what dies is his kingdom, leaving the way clear for the new kingdom for Cronus. From the blood of Uranus are born the Erinyes, as a symbol of Cronus' guilt. Cronus signifies time and symbolises the devouring greed of humans, animals, and love, an insatiable desire of evolution.

Zeus puts the universe in definitive order. This is the beginning of spirituality and the new order that is to follow with the generation of Olympian gods. Cronus stands against Mnemosyne, who represents memory. Metis, who is prudence and who has magic powers, prepares the potion to make Uranus vomit. She is later Zeus' first wife.

All men need gods.

Homer

2. THE WAR OF THE TITANS

A bloody war was unleashed that lasted ten years, and battles raged from the high summits of the sky to the depths of Tartarus. The Titans and some of their children were more numerous and driven by their fury against Zeus and his followers, which included the Oceanid Styx and her numerous children alongside Zeus' siblings. In exchange for her help, Styx received the privilege that the gods swore in his name, which gave the oath absolute value.

Zeus considered his forces and those opposing him, and he decided to seek further help. Then he remembered the Cyclops and the Hecatoncheires, who were still imprisoned in Tartarus, forgotten by all. Zeus descended cautiously into Tartarus and killed Kampe, the jailer, took his keys and freed his brothers, giving them food and divine drink to fortify them. The Cyclops gave Zeus the lightning bolt in gratitude; they gave Hades the helmet of darkness; and to Poseidon they gave a trident.

The three armed brothers formed a plan to bring the war, which had gone on too long already, to a swift end. And so Hades went unseen into the presence of the twisted Cronus and stole his weapons, while Poseidon diverted his attention by threatening him with the trident. And finally, Zeus struck him with his terrible lightning. Meanwhile, the giant Hecatoncheires hurled hundreds of rocks at the other Titans, who were forced to flee in defeat. The cruel war of the Titans was known as 'Titanomachy', in memory of these giants. And Cronus and all the Titans that followed him were sent down into Tartarus and guarded by the Hecantoncheires, except for Atlas, who being the force's leader received an exemplary punishment: he was condemned to bear the weight of the world on his shoulders forever.

An analysis of the myth of Atlas

It is also told that Perseus sought hospitality from Atlas and was refused. Angered, the hero showed him Medusa's head, which he had cut off, and the giant was petrified by the horror of the head and was converted into a mountain, which supported the vault of heaven and gave him his name.

Thus, Atlas is the symbol of the strength that bears the universe, and the word was adopted first for geographical atlases and then for the main mountain chain of southern Maghreb, owing to its size and height in relation to the great expanse of desert that surrounds it. Lastly, in anatomy the first vertebra of the neck, on which rests the weight of the head, is also called the Atlas. It is also worth mentioning that Voltaire associated Newton, who compiled the laws of gravity, with Atlas.

Zeus divided his kingdom between his siblings, as had his father: he gave Poseidon the sea, Hades the Underworld, and he kept the skies for himself, ruling over Earth and the Heavens from Mount Olympus. The three kingdoms were independent from each other, and not even Zeus had any power over Hades and Poseidon.

Analysis and comments

Zeus' victory increased his power to an absolute power over the world, and brought an end to the powerful deities and disordered forces that, like Cronus, had destroyed and corrupted everything in their path. The Greeks saw Cronus as the force that corrupted humans and animals (the corpses). For philosophers, this triumph symbolises the victory of order and reason over instinct and passion.

> *Happy he that has acquired the wealth of the divine*
> *Knowledge, wretched he who has*
> *A dark opinion of the Gods.*

Empedocles of Agrigentum

3. PROMETHEUS AND THE ORIGINS OF HUMANITY

Prometheus was the son of the Titan *Iapetus* and the nymph *Clymene*, daughter of Tethys and Oceanus. Unlike his brothers, *Atlas* and *Menoetius*, Prometheus, much more wisely, joined the ranks of Zeus and persuaded *Epimetheus* to do the same.

When Pallas Athena saw how intelligent he was, she decided to instruct him in architecture, astronomy, mathematics, navigation, medicine, and other useful arts. And Zeus, therefore, put him in charge of creating humankind, to share the world with the animals and plants.

So Prometheus took a lump of clay, mixed it with water, a created the first man in the image of the gods. Eros breathed the spirit of life onto the model, and Athena gave it a soul, and the figure came to life.

Prometheus was satisfied with his work. He loved it so much that he only wanted the best for it. So one day, after sacrificing an ox, he made two piles: the largest contained the bones and the fat covered by the animal's skin and the other its meat. He asked Zeus to choose one, and he chose the larger. Angered and offended by the trick, he refused to give fire to the humans, which was the special possession of the gods, and which Prometheus had requested for humanity.

Then he went to Athena, who felt sympathy for him and decided to help, letting him into Olympus. Carefully, Prometheus stole a spark which he put in a hollow cane. He left as stealthily as he had come, and give the fire to man.

The fire, essential for cooking food, sacrifices, and for the humans' work, was Prometheus' gift, and with it he not only saved humanity from cold and hunger, but also helped the progress of technology.

However, his act angered Zeus, who swore vengeance, first on Prometheus and then on humanity. From his high throne on the peaks of Mount Olympus, he stretched out his arm and grasped the offender in his powerful grip, and took him to the Caucasus mountains and tied him to a rock, where a vulture picked out his liver bit by bit, causing intolerable pain. During the night, while the vulture slept, his liver and guts reformed to be devoured over and over again.

Analysis of the myth

Prometheus is the myth that has been given most literary and artistic representation. Basically, it tells of humanity's fight against weakness; the struggle of the weakest against the authority imposed for its own benefit or, in other words, the fight between humanity and the divine. It represents humanity as ambitious, intelligent, anti-conformist, and active – a people who try to achieve equality with the gods.

The basis of the legend and the explanation of its extraordinary fortune are captured in Hesiod's *Works and Days*: Prometheus' relation to the birth of the human race. The giant represents anti-tyranny, by standing against the wrath of Zeus, and the force that permits the emancipation of humanity from the yoke of fate. In the fifties, people started to talk a great deal about humans and promethean humanism. Existentialists take Prometheus as a symbol of rebellion against metaphysical and religious order and the personification of the rejection of the absurdity of the human condition. Prometheus, in giving humanity fire and civilisation, opened the doors of progress and the way to freedom. According to Plato, Prometheus is the symbol of progress.

The comparisons of this myth with the Christian religion are very interesting: Prometheus appeared as the fallen angel, struck down by the wrath of Yahweh for offering humanity the fruit of the tree of science, or knowledge. The followers of Lucifer believe that he was called Lux-fer, because his hand carries the flaming torch, with the flame of the sanctuary vault. This parallelism is more surprising if we remember that Prometheus was the creator of humans. Another interpretation tells that Prometheus was placed on the cross, like Christ, for the denial of the love of humans, while the suffering of the Titan in Caucasus represents the passion and the agony of Christ. Some authors see Christ as the new Prometheus who dies for humanity, and there are those who believe that Prometheus symbolises the cycle of life.

Prometheus is sent to Mount Caucasus, the easternmost part of the known world, exactly the opposite to his brother Atlas, who was exiled to the westernmost part.

In Aeschylus' work *Prometheus Bound*, he calls the friend of humanity a philanthropist, and in J. J. Rousseau's *Discourse on the Arts and Sciences*, written in 1750, Prometheus, instead of being humanity's benefactor, corrupts it by introducing the perspective of knowledge and technology.

According to the psychoanalytical concepts, Prometheus represents the awakening of conscience and intellectuality, the maturity of freed humanity as no longer dependent on higher powers.

> *In exchange for fire, I will give*
> *man an evil that all will enjoy,*
> *revelling in their own downfall.*

Zeus

4. PANDORA. THE FIRST WOMAN

Once Zeus had punished Prometheus, he had to think about what would be the best punishment for man, who had accepted the gift from his benefactor. He ordered Hephaestus to fabricate a woman from clay, the Four Winds to breathe life into her, and all the gods to adorn her.

Athena gave her light green eyes; the divine Charities decorated her with golden necklaces; the Horae gave her a beautiful mane of hair; and Hermes, in his indiscretion, gave her the gift of lies, seductive words, and volubility. The woman was called Pandora, which means 'all gift' or 'all gifts': 'Pan' signifying all, and 'Dora' gifts. Before she was given to the human race, Zeus gave her a box.

Hermes carried her to Epimetheus, as a gift from the sky. Though his brother Prometheus had warned man not to accept any gifts from Zeus, man was gullible and happily took the woman and married her. It is said that Epimetheus was somewhat slow and candid by nature.

But Epimetheus' days of happiness were not to last much longer, as one day Pandora gave in to the temptation of looking inside the box that Zeus had given her. Overcome by curiosity, she opened the lid and immediately all the bad spirits: old age, hunger, disease, poverty, madness, and all their companions flew out and were dispersed throughout the world. However, Zeus must have had some pity for the human race, for at the bottom of the box, Pandora found Hope, the saviour of the human race.

Other authors believe the box (which was also said to be a chest tied with a thousand knots) was filled with divine gifts that, when freed, abandoned humanity and returned to Olympus.

Analysis of the myth

As we have seen, Prometheus' intervention was fundamental in the mythical explanation of the essential institutions of society: the sacrifice, fire as the origin of culture and progress. In the same way, the arrival of Pandora, an artificial and refined divine invention, is the mythical vision of matrimony and the appearance of evil in the world. Pandora is Eve, the first biblical woman, who brought about humanity's perdition with her curiosity. However, she was created in a much more subtle way and was perfectly finished and beautiful. Even so both legends create the image of woman as curious and incisive.

The conclusion of the myth leaves certain unanswered questions: why was Hope in the box along with all the evils? Rather than resulting from Zeus's pity, was Hope not an evil along with all the rest? Would it be better if humanity was without hope? And why was it squashed in at the bottom? Was it so weighted down, when usually it is considered light and free?

According to the Ancients, evil entered the world, bearing intolerable misery; but at the same time, Hope was always nearby, to help humanity and ensure that a happy future was always possible.

Times of success sustained by a silver age,
Surpassing the bronze, but surpassed again
By gold.

Ovid

5. THE FIVE AGES OF HUMANITY

The first race created by humanity, beginning with that modelled by Prometheus, lived in the so-called *Golden Age*. This race lived without ills in a sort of Eden, where unlimited fruit grew from the leafy trees. These people danced and sang in merriment, ignorant of disease and old age and with no fear of death. It is said that, in time, they all perished, to become spirits of good fortune and justice. The following race, also a divine creation, was not so fortunate. This was the *Silver Age*, less prosperous, in which humans had to work to feed themselves. It was the age when humanity came to know and appreciate the seasons of the year and also the cold. Even so, they were still happier than their descendants, who lived during the *Bronze Age*, when fighting became customary, and differences were resolved with violence. Each and every one of this race was taken by the plague.

The fourth race lived in the second part of the Bronze Age, also called the *Age of Heroes*, and was noble and generous, as it is said that they were engendered between gods and mortal women. They fought gloriously in Thebes, in the voyage of the Argonauts, and in the Trojan War, and were converted into a race of heroes, inhabiting Elysium.

The fifth race was the race that prospered, the indigenous descendants of the fourth. They were degenerate, cruel, unjust, malicious, lustful, ungrateful children and traitors. This was the *Iron Age*, and was by far the worst: wars broke out incessantly, the rights of hospitality were openly violated, and there were constant rapes, murders, and robberies.

Analysis and comments

The Greeks observed the specific events of their own history, and created this myth about the origin and evolution of humanity. The poet Hesiod wrote about the five ages that humanity lived through until his era. Unlike Ovid, Hesiod never wrote about the Great Flood.

During the Golden Age, humans lived in an ideal world

of justice and perfection, which the Christians later identified with Paradise. The Silver Age reflects the matriarchal society of remote times, when woman was the centre of society and man worked with her in agricultural labour. The Bronze Age was the period of the first Greek conquests, the last examples of which are the warrior kings of Mycenaean. The Age of Heroes lasted only a brief period, due to the devastation caused by the numerous wars, which Homer used as the setting for the heroes of *The Iliad*. The Iron Age corresponds to the period of Dorian supremacy, the Greek society that began around the twelfth century BC. The Dorians already dominated iron and its use in fabricating weapons, and they destroyed the Mycenaean civilisation.

> *Hills and valleys no longer know distinction,*
> *Uniform nature remains below, oppressed;*
> *The majority of mortals perish in the Flood.*

> Ovid

6. THE GREAT FLOOD

From his kingdom on Mount Olympus, Zeus observed the evolution of humanity, and he did not like what he saw. His wrath at the impious sons of Lycaon, sons of Pelasgos, reached such a height that he decided to annihilate them.

First he thought of roasting them with the fire from his lightning, but another god dissuaded him from this method, saying that the flames could reach Olympus. Finally he decided to wipe humanity from the Earth with a great flood. He sought the help of the Four Winds, who united enough clouds to provoke an almighty storm when they were struck by his terrible lightning. Poseidon brandished his trident with such might that he created enormous waves, uniting with the storm to flood the world.

The unfortunate humans, terrified at the deluge, forgot their fights in a vain attempt to escape from the floods. They climbed mountains, reaching the highest summits, but it was useless, for the waters continued to rise, catching them one by one, drowning their last despairing screams and swallowing their homes and villages, where they could have lived in happiness and peace, under ferocious waves.

Analysis of the myth

We can see the parallel between Zeus and Yahweh with respect to humanity and its decisions: "Yahweh, seeing that the evil of man on earth was great, and that the thoughts of all tended constantly to evil, regretted the creation of man on earth and his heart grieved so that he said: 'I will exterminate the race that I have formed from the face of the earth...' (Genesis VI, lines 5-6) and send them a great flood."

The notion of the flood is common to almost all religions, both Eastern and Western. We find it in the Bible, in Gilgamesh's epic, and in Greek and Roman mythology. The most probable explanation is that the idea of eradication by flood came after an unmeasured catastrophe caused by the rivers Tigris and Euphrates. The flood, the result of divine wrath, was sent to punish the humans of the Bronze Age, according to some authors, and of the Iron Age, according to others, so that humanity might be reborn in a purified from. In Greek history, the evolution of the myth supposes that human civilisation had reached a high level, after which it began a moral decline.

> *Who does not see the name of Deucalion fleeing,*
> *When the Earth, its men and the sea*
> *Had lost its shore*
> *Old Noah!*

> Fletcher

7. DEUCALION AND PYRRHA

And the rain continued to fall incessantly until, after several days, the water covered the entire surface of the Earth, except for Mount Parnassus, the highest peak in Greece. It was there that Deucalion, son of Prometheus, and his faithful wife Pyrrha, daughter of Epimetheus and Pandora, had taken refuge from the flood that was all around them. The couple had always been good and virtuous, even when surrounded by the depravation of their neighbours, and they had always worshipped Zeus faithfully. So Zeus took pity on them and saved them from the flood. He ordered the winds to return to their caves and the rain to cease, and Poseidon calmed the waters and recalled the errant waves.

When peace was returned to Earth, Deucalion and Pyrrha looked around them disconsolately, not knowing what to do. They decided to go to the sanctuary of Delphi, which had been strong enough to resist the force of the deluge, and went to find out the will of the gods. Themis appeared to them in person, and said: "Cover your heads and drag the bones of your mother behind!"

At first, the two were horrified by these words, but as both their mothers were dead, they decided that Themis must be referring to the Earth, whose bones were the rocks that lay on the bank of the river. The husband and wife decided to act straight away. Covering their heads, they descended, dragging the rocks down after them. All the rocks that Deucalion dragged were converted into men, and all those that Pyrrha dragged became women. In this way the earth was re-populated with a race of innocent men and women. Shortly afterwards, Deucalion and Pyrrha had Hellen, who was later to give his name to the Hellenic or Greek race.

Analysis of the myth

There is another version sustained by some mythologists, though it is not as popular or accepted by the Greeks as is their traditional version. It tells that Deucalion, king of Thessaly, was warned by his father Prometheus of the forthcoming flood and built an ark, stocking it with supplies, and boarded it with his wife Pyrrha. The ark was afloat for many days and eventually ran aground on the summit of Mount

Parnassus. This version is much closer to the version of Noah's ark that appears in the Bible and presents divine punishment for evil and piety for the virtuous.

III

THE GODS OF OLYMPUS

He, whose omnipresent eyes contemplate the world;
He, eternal Thunder, seated on a golden throne;
He makes the sky thunder with his feet,
And beneath him all Olympus trembles.

Homer

1. ZEUS, KING OF THE GODS

Zeus was the father of all of the gods, the king of Olympus, the most powerful and venerated god. He was the god of thunder and lightning, the supreme governor of the universe, the personification of the sky, and the guardian of political order and peace. He was the most prominent of all the deities of Olympus, and all the rest were forced to submit to his will.

For the pre-Socratic philosophers, it was Zeus who opened the way of reason to humans and taught them that real knowledge is only obtained through *pain*. Zeus could not intervene in personal decisions, as each person must go

49

through their own personal experiences alone, and he was limited exclusively to rewarding sincere efforts and punishing impious behaviour. For all these attributes, Homer defined him as the first god and the supreme lord of mortals, as well as the father of the gods and humans – not genetically or emotionally, but in the general idea of a father who sustains and protects his family against war, plagues, and other catastrophes.

His supremacy was only questioned once, when Hera, Apollo, Poseidon, and the other gods, except Hestia, surrounded and bound him while he slept. But the Nereid Tethys, fearing civil war, called the Hecatoncheires Briareus, who untied the hundred knots quickly with his hundred hands. Zeus took revenge on the instigator of the conspiracy, Hera, by hanging her from the sky by golden bracelets on each wrist, with anvils tied to her ankles. The others did not dare to get her down, fearful of Zeus' wrath, despite her pitiful cries. Finally, Zeus agreed to take her down, provided they all swore never to rebel against him again. He punished Apollo and Poseidon for their part in the conspiracy by sending them as slaves to King Laomedon, for whom they built the city of Troy.

Zeus was the personification of the sky and all phenomena of the air, and the guardian of political order and peace. In order to ensure the continuation of his lineage, he had sexual relationships with several of the Titans, as well as with his sisters and other deities. These unions produced numerous offspring, for example, with Metis, the Reason, he had Athena; with Themis he had the Moirae and the Seasons; with Mnemosyne he had the Muses; with Demeter he had Persephone; with Eurynome he had the Charities; and with Leto, or Latona, he had Apollo and Artemis.

However, the only woman he wed was Hera, who came to be accepted as his legitimate wife of Zeus and the most important goddess of all. But at first, Hera refused Zeus and tried to flee him. He pursued her over Knossos, in Crete, or according to others, over Mount Thornax in Argolis, where again his wooing was unsuccessful. So Zeus came up with a plan and disguised himself as a cuckoo covered in mud. Hera, on seeing the poor bird, took pity on him and held him

Zeus.

against her breast to warm him. Then Zeus returned to his true form and raped her, after which Hera felt shamed into marrying him.

In spite of the circumstances, the wedding was quite an event, attended by all the gods, who all brought wedding presents. Among the presents was the tree of golden apples that Mother Earth gave to Hera, which later was put under the care of the Hesperides in Hera's garden on Mount Atlas. It is said their wedding night was spent in Samos and lasted for three hundred years. Hera conceived four deities: *Ares, Hephaestus, Hebe,* and *Eileithyia.* Under the excuse of ensuring his bloodline, Zeus turned out to be an unfaithful husband, easily led by his desires and having relations with many mortal women, which produced a race of heroes and demi-gods. In this way, Zeus assured himself of a sort of hierarchy that would always give him the advantage of power over gods and men.

The mythological tales about Zeus are innumerable, but perhaps he is best known for his countless love affairs. The number of children he engendered is more than fifty – both legitimate and illegitimate, for which reason almost all the great bloodlines of Ancient Greece considered him their father and founder.

Some of his relationships are notable for the tragic circumstances that surround his targets, as Zeus employed all means of cunning, taking forms as diverse as humans, animals, and others to conquer his desired objectives. Of all these adventures, only one homosexual affair is known, with the Trojan Ganymede. Zeus kidnapped him by taking the shape of an eagle (the symbol of royalty), with powerful wings and keen sight. He carried Ganymede in his talons to Olympus, where he made him his personal wine and nectar pourer.

So that all the Greeks could contemplate his splendour, Zeus had a magnificent monument built: the famous colossal statue of the Olympian Zeus of Phidias, which was finished in the year 456 BC. The Greeks owe many of their exquisite statues of the gods to Phidias, but none equals the size, the dignity, or the outstanding elaboration of the splendid figure of Zeus. Sculpted of marble and ebony and richly adorned with precious stones and gold, it appears to have stood fifteen metres tall. It showed the father of the gods frowning down on his kingdom, for the Greeks said that when Zeus frowned, Olympus would tremble. He is surrounded by his everyday attributes and symbols: the eagle, lightning, and victory, in a permanent tribute to the grand supremacy of his status as the king of all. It is told that Phidias, on finishing the statue, begged the approval of Zeus himself. In answer to his pleas, the great god sent down a brilliant lightning bolt that bounced off the ground all around the colossal image, without damaging one detail. This masterpiece of Olympus, which tragically disappeared, is one of the Seven Wonders of the World, along with the lighthouse of Alexandria and the Colossus of Rhodes.

Analysis of the god Zeus

Zeus was a more terrible god than the others, but several centuries of history, myths, and varied traditions have established him as the most important of the gods. After many years of worshipping different gods, the Greeks needed an all-powerful divine being in order to create a hierarchy amongst the god, and that place was filled by Zeus. The reason for his high status was that he was the god of the atmospheric conditions, who filled the sky with clouds or cleared it; launched lightning, and caused the thunder to roll. In lands that were mostly dependent on agriculture, a god with such power over the uncontrollable elements, which could make or break a harvest, could only become a highly venerated figure. Zeus germinated the idea of *paternity*. With the territorial, economic, and social expansion the Greeks achieved, families were grouped together in villages, called *demos*. The *demos* were united under city states, *polis*. Each family unit was under the authority of patriarchal rule, and the man of the family imposed the laws of the land on his family subjects.

Zeus was the father of the gods, and as their king he ruled over both gods and men, and constituted the model for all Greek patriarchs. As head of the family, Zeus believed the growth of his clan took precedence over his duties as a faithful husband to Hera. He carried out his *paternal duties* in any way he was able, with both goddesses and mortal women. All the regions and cities of Greece considered it an honour to have a son of Zeus as their patron or founder.

JUPITER, THE KING OF THE SKY AND THE EARTH

For the ancient Roman civilisation, Jupiter was the most important of their gods in the same way that Zeus was for the Greeks. He was considered, apart from the king of the gods and the personification of the sky and the elements, the absolute and supreme power of the entire universe. His dominion over the atmospheric phenomena, including rain, storms, and daylight earned him various names, such as "Fulgurator", "Pluvius", "Tonans", "Tonitrualis", and "Fulminator". As time passed, he was attributed the characteristics and powers of smaller local gods, while their representations acquired new strengths and diverse forms. Only Hades, the Moirae, and Fate dared to contradict his will and continued to impose their irrevocable decrees. The other gods carried out Zeus' orders and submitted to his will. Jupiter was accustomed to call all the gods to meet when it was necessary to discuss an important matter with them or sometimes simply to enjoy a sumptuous banquet of nectar and ambrosia.

Like any ruler, Jupiter had his special assistants, such as *Nike*, the goddess of victory, who was always by his side and at his command. It was said that her love and respect for Jupiter was such that she used to carry an image of him in her hands. *Fama*, the Latin deity who was the personification of fame and the goddess of the hundred tongues, proclaimed all that Jupiter desired with a blast on her trumpet, never questioning whether the desire was true or false. Other gods that assisted Jupiter were the goddess *Fortune*, who is sometimes seen close to Jupiter balancing on a continually turning wheel, whose thoughtless hands take from some and throw gifts to others. Juventas, her daughter and the goddess of Youth, was the royal nectar server until she was replaced by Ganymede.

As the personification of the sky, Jupiter married Juno (Atmosphere) and had romances with other goddesses such as Themis (Justice), Dione (Humanity), and Ceres, (Tierra), as well as mortal women, such as Europa and Danae. The Romans accepted Jupiter's polygamy, as they considered these unions symbolic.

The legend of Juturna

This is one of the few legends attributed to Jupiter. It tells of how the god fell hopelessly in love with *Juturna*, also called Yuturna and Diuturna, who was the sister of King Turnus of the Rutulians. Juturna was a nymph of a spring in Lazio and was famous in Roman mythology for her incredible beauty and for remaining unaffected by the desire and pleas of her lord Jupiter. Instead of punishing her for her refusal to submit to his will, he granted her immortality and the power to reign over the waves. Soon the frozen water of the beautiful nymph's spring became famous for its healing properties and came to represent her insensitivity to Jupiter's passion.

* * *

The Roman state was very centralised and needed an all-powerful god who would strengthen unity on social and political grounds as well as religious. Jupiter, therefore, became a type of political god, standing for the guarantee if law and order, agreements and oaths, as well as the protector of the state and the power responsible for the victory of foreign campaigns.

Jupiter's importance to the state of Rome did not suffer, unlike the roles of other gods, with the incorporation of his Greek counterpart Zeus into the Roman pantheon. Though Jupiter enjoyed the fame of borrowed legends, he continued to hold an important position in both politics and religion until the end of paganism. He formed a link between the cities of the Empire, which possessed a temple and statues dedicated to the god. His most important temples, like the Capitolium in Rome, where Jupiter, Juno, and Minerva formed the Capitoline Triad, the protectors of the unity of the city, and the Sanctuary of Jupiter Ammon in Libya, were known worldwide. He also had a temple in Dodona, where an oak tree foretold mysterious prophecies, supposedly inspired by Jupiter himself. This sanctuary was thought lost for many centuries and has recently been rediscovered.

Jupiter bore different names according to who invoked him and for what purpose. To stop an invasion, Jupiter Stator was invoked, as occurred a great deal during the period of conflict between the Romans and the Sabines. The remains of the enemy leaders were offered to Jupiter Feretrio. The Roman councils, when they requested his assistance, made their pleas to Optimus Maximus, who also protected the emperors, who often passed themselves off as his bloodline or adopted his titles for themselves in order to further their prestige.

Hera, who presides
Supreme over brides and grooms.

Virgil

2. HERA, THE JEALOUS WIFE

Hera was the queen of the sky and goddess of the elements and matrimony. She represented nobility, bordering on hermetism, and had been educated by Oceanus and Tethys, the parents of the Oceanids. In historic times, she was responsible for the tutelage of newly-born children, and in all the legends regarding Zeus, she is his sacred wife. She was possibly the personification of Mother Earth, who rose above her terrestrial nature when she became Zeus' wife.

Her happy marriage came to an end when her husband revealed his inclination for being unfaithful to her with other goddesses, and even with mortal women. This drove

Hera to become jealous and vindictive, and her continuous fights with her husband were famous. She took her husband's constant infidelity as a grave offence and, never backing down, pursued and cruelly punished both her husband's lovers and the children born of these unions. It is said that the real reason that Hera conspired with Apollo and Poseidon against Zeus was so that he could not descend to the earth and meet with his lovers.

However, Hera was also desired by many mortal men, such as the giants *Porphyrius* and *Ixion*. Zeus showed himself to be more jealous than she, sending a lightning bolt down on the former and condemning the latter to eternal punishment. Hera often intervened in human affairs, as she was the only god who had equal power to that of her husband, for she could grant the gift of prophecy to humans and beasts. In this way, she helped the Greeks in their fight against the Trojans to avenge Paris and protected the Argonauts on their voyage on board the *Argo*, when they passed through the Scylla and Charybdis.

In spite of her great power, Hera could never use the title "Queen of the Gods and Humans", as she was considered simply the wife of the supreme deity, though she was worshipped by all.

The creation of the peacock is attributed to Hera, in memory of *Argos*, the hundred-eyed giant. With his terrible strength, the giant performed many tasks for Hera, such as killing a rampaging bull that was creating devastation in the region of Arcadia or when he killed the monster Echidna. These feats were appreciated by Hera, and she took the giant as her servant and charged him with the task of keeping a permanent watch on Io, one of Zeus' lovers. When Zeus found out, he ordered Hermes to kill the giant, and Hera greatly felt the loss of such a loyal and devoted servant. She took his hundred eyes and placed them on the plumage of the elegant bird. Argos also was given the name 'Pan Optes' (he who sees all).

Iris, the Rainbow, was her most faithful servant after Argos, and just as Zeus had Hermes, Iris was the swift and trustworthy messenger of Hera. It is said that she flew so rapidly through the air that she was hardly visible. Only the shining trail left across the sky by her multi-coloured cloak showed her passing. Iris was Hera's bridge between the sky and the Earth.

Analysis of the goddess Hera

The cult dedicated to the worship of Hera is similar to that of Cybele in Phrygia, Asia Minor, as both were considered the nurturer and protector of all females. Hera is the prototype of the faithful wife, an unfailingly honest wife constantly deceived by her husband, but she does not represent the figure of *mother*. In her relationship with Zeus, she takes the most normal and coherent attitude toward her marriage, demanding unconditional love from her husband and refusing to accept his infidelity. Hera is defined as the defender of monogamy, preaching the acceptance of a single man as the companion and complement of his wife. When her idea of matrimonial fidelity was not fulfilled, she abandoned Olympus to punish and humiliate the lovers of her husband. Zeus, on the other hand, never managed to understand his wife's possessive behaviour, as his most important objective was to engender offspring, and he did not believe this had to be accomplished with just one woman. According to Demosthenes, men have wives in order to bear them children, and they have concubines to give them pleasure.

For the Greeks, Hera was also the goddess of legitimate matrimony, as she was the only one of the deities who was legitimately married. She was also the goddess of fecundity and, together with her daughter Eileithyia, the protector of women in birth. In both literature and art, she is represented with the traditional attributes of her sceptre and crown. Her face, hidden behind several veils, symbolises marriage, and she sometimes is shown holding a grenadine, symbol of fecundity, in her hand.

Her attitude, strict and moralist, is explained by the historical period which she occupied. The cult of the goddess was founded at the time when the Greeks were in the process of adopting democracy and monogamy and required an exemplary divinity who would punish any transgressions.

JUNO, THE CONSORT GODDESS

The goddess Juno was worshipped in Rome as the wife of Jupiter and the queen of the skies. Etymologically, the name Juno comes from the same root as the name Jupiter. The goddess is described as a great woman, beautiful and majestic, enrobed in flowing tunics, a crown on her head and the sceptre in her hand. Both the peacock and the cuckoo were her sacred animals and are often represented at her side.

Above all, Juno protected the Roman woman. She accompanied her in the course of her daily life, from birth until death. Her role was that of a double divinity, which meant that each woman had her own personal Juno protector, just as each man had his own personal guardian. She would be given a different name depending on her stage of life and the role performed. Thus, when she presided over a marriage she was called Jugalis; but women in labour called on the help of Juno Lucina. New born babies were also put under her protection, for which reason she was considered, rather then the goddess of marriage, the supreme matron of mothers and bore the name Juno Matronalia.

The festivities carried out in Rome in her honour were occasions of great pomp and ceremony. The main temples dedicated to Hera were in Mycenae, Sparta, and Argos, and those for the worship of Juno were in Rome and Hereum. There were also many smaller temples dedicated to her in other cities, where less important festivals were celebrated.

Juno was not as important as her Greek counterpart, however, she was closer to the humans than Hera. Above all, she was the testimony of the power of the fertility of women, and she also formed part of the Capitoline Triad, alongside Jupiter and Minerva, which preserved the Roman state and assured its continuance.

The beautiful has been born, and the land and sea
Will worship the hour of this mysterious birth.

Shelley

3. APHRODITE, THE BEAUTIFUL GODDESS OF THE SEA

The goddess of beauty, love, laughter, and matrimony also was known as Venus by the Romans, and sometimes as Dione or Cythera. Her powers were far reaching: as a gentle, kind goddess, she protected marriages, favoured understanding and love between spouses, brought fertility to the household, and presided over women in labour. But the other side of Aphrodite was a terrible goddess who symbolised unleashed passion and drove lovers mad with desire. She also caused marital problems by inciting adultery and favouring fertility in illicit love affairs.

There are two different versions of the story of Aphrodite's birth. The first tells that she was the daughter of Zeus and Dione, one of the goddesses of the first divine generation of Ancient Greece. According to the second, more poetic version, Aphrodite was conceived from the sperm that fell into the sea when Cronus mutilated Uranus. The sperm fertilised the waves and from them, the goddess emerged, as white and perfect as the white foam on the tips of the waves. She floated to the island of Cythera, but as it was very small, she continued to Peloponnesus and finally settled in Paphos, Cyprus, which continued to be the principal seat of her cult. Where she emerged from the sea and stepped onto the land, flowers, and plants sprouted from the ground. The four lovely *Horae*, the Seasons, daughters of Zeus and Themis and sisters of the Charities, were awaiting her arrival to decorate her and adorn her beautiful, naked body.

Her entourage was made up of *Eros* (the god of love), *Himeros* (desire), and *Hymen* (marriage), and when she

Aphrodite.

arrived in Olympus, a throne and all the gods were awaiting her, enraptured by her beauty, so much so that they all proposed marriage to her. But she refused them all with disdain. Zeus, one of the hopefuls, ordered that as a punishment she marry Hephaestus, the deformed son of Hera and god of the forge.

The enforced marriage was not a happy one, as Aphrodite was soon unfaithful to her husband with his brother Ares, the god of war, with whom she had the goddess Harmony, as well as Deimos (the god of terror) and Phobos (the god of dread), both characteristics inherited from their father. One day, Hephaestus surprised the lovers and imprisoned them under a golden net, calling all the other gods to witness their dishonour. Only the gods came; the goddesses preferred, for delicacy's sake, to stay in their dominions. Hephaestus proclaimed that he would only set the couple free if the wedding gifts he had given to Zeus were returned, but Zeus refused. Apollo asked Hermes if he would mind exchanging places with Ares, and the god, dazzled by Aphrodite's beauty, swore he would. Poseidon suggested to Hephaestus that Ares buy his freedom by paying the equivalent of the wedding gifts and offered to marry Aphrodite himself. Finally, Ares was set free and returned to Thrace; Aphrodite left Olympus to spend some time on Pathos, abandoned and ashamed. It is said that there she renewed her virginity in the sea.

Grateful to the gods that had helped her, Aphrodite first slept with Hermes, by whom she bore a son, Hermaphrodite, then with Poseidon, by whom she gave birth to two sons, Rhodos and Herophilos, and lastly with Apollo, with whom she had Pryapus, an ugly child with huge genitals.

Not content with her relationships with the gods, Aphrodite also had various affairs with mortals. One theory states, however, that this was a punishment set by Zeus for her arrogance. The Trojan Anchises, for example, was ensnared by her beauty, and with him she had *Aeneas*, an ancestor of the family of Julia, from which Caesar claimed to be a descendant.

The myth of Adonis

It is said that the wife of King Kinryas of Cyprus once boasted that her daughter Smyrna was much more beautiful than Aphrodite. The goddess was insulted and avenged her wrath on Smyrna by making her fall in love with her father and fooled him into sleeping with her. When the king discovered that he was both the father and the grandfather of the baby Smyrna was expecting, he became so furious that he took up a sword. Aphrodite was ashamed of the problems she had caused and turned Smyrna into a myrrh tree, which the powerful sword chopped into two and from which emerged *Adonis*.

Aphrodite hid Adonis in a chest and gave him to Persephone, the wife of Hades and daughter of Demeter, to look after. The queen of the Dead was curious about Aphrodite's secret and opened the chest to discover Adonis. Taken by his beauty, she released him and brought him up in her palace. When Aphrodite found out, she ran to Tartarus to reclaim Adonis, and when Persephone refused, she went to Zeus for help. But Zeus preferred not to act as judge in such a matter and passed the case to the minor tribunal, presided over by the muse Calliope. She gave the verdict that Adonis should spend a third of the year with Aphrodite, a third with Persephone, and the remaining third as he chose. But Aphrodite, not satisfied with the judge's decision, seduced Adonis with a magic girdle and persuaded him to spend the third that corresponded to his own wish with her as well.

Persephone avenged this act by going to Thrace, where she told Ares that Aphrodite preferred Adonis to him. Ares, mad with jealousy, turned himself into a wild boar and attacked Adonis, who was killed. Where his blood was spilled, anemones sprung up, the first and ephemeral flower of spring, and his soul descended to Tartarus. From the wounds that Aphrodite suffered when she went to his aid and was scratched by brambles, the blood stained the white roses red. Aphrodite was grief stricken, and begged Zeus to allow her lover to leave Tartarus during the summer months to spend them with her, which Zeus conceded.

Analysis of the myth of Adonis

The symbolism of a myth is never as evident as in that of Adonis. He is the vegetation that descends to the kingdom of the dead to be reunited with Persephone, then returns to the earth in spring to be with his love and to give flowers and fruit in the summer. He represents the unceasing cycle of the death and resurrection of nature. This myth originated in Syria and, before reaching, Greece was modified in Egypt and Cyprus.

Analysis of the goddess Aphrodite

She was called Aphrodite by humans and gods, as she was born from the spray of the waves (*aphros* in Greek), and she was also called Cythera and Cyprogenia, as she was born from the waves of Cyprus.

The goddess, because of her sensual character, is assimilated with the Phoenician goddess *Astarte*, the mother of fertility. This theory is supported by the fact that Aphrodite was not born like the rest of the gods, but emerged from the spray of the sea, fertilised by the sexual organs of Uranus after his castration. Neither is it a coincidence that the eastern goddess appears in Cyprus, an area influenced by the Ancient Phoenicians. The Semitic goddess Astarte is always represented with a young god, her lover, whose rituals were readapted with the rationalised inclusion of the myth of Adonis, who died and was revived on the third day, according to Phoenician legend. Even so, the mental perception of the Greeks could not easily accept the irrational elements of the new divinity, and thus invented a rebirth, with a genealogy similar to that of other immortals. Zeus and Dione, who according to tradition was the daughter of either Oceanus and Tethys or Cronus and Gaea (though her name is no more than the feminine of the Greek for 'god'), became the parents of the goddess of unearthly beauty. As a result of this, Aphrodite is the most significant case of the adaptation and recreation of a foreign myth by the rational and logical mind of Greek society.

Persephone.

Aphrodite is probably the deity who has inspired the most paintings and sculptures. She is generally represented naked or semi-naked, in voluptuous poses, and with a fine veil around her full and beautiful figure. She often appears with Adonis or Eros (Cupid to the Romans). From the many artists who illustrated her, such as Titian, Cranach, Giorgione, and Praxiteles, only Botticelli has represented her birth in the beautiful "Birth of Venus".

VENUS, THE MOST BEAUTIFUL OF ALL

The goddess of the ancient Roman society did not have much importance in her origins. She protected the fertile earth and ensured the blossoming of flowers and the production of fruit. It was after the second century BC, when she was assimilated with the Greek goddess Aphrodite and took on her characteristics, legends, and attributes, that she became more important and achieved notable authority in Roman society. A century later, Julius Caesar, the great Roman emperor, attributed the origins of his ancestors to the 'gens Julia' and Aeneas, son of Anchises and Venus, fixed the cult of those who he claimed had forged his roots.

Venus rose from a minor deity to the great goddess of beauty, love, laughter, and matrimony. She protected young lovers and helped them in their romantic adventures, such as in the story of Hero and Leander. Venus' assistants were *Himeros*, the god of amorous desire; *Pothos*, the god of the friendships of love; *Suadela*, the god of the soft words of love; Hymen, the god of marriage; and Cupid, the winged god and personification of intense desire. Cupid shot his burning arrows of love at the targets that Venus ordered. In this sense, his power and intervention in Roman mythology were much more important than those of Eros in Greek mythology, with whom he was assimilated.

According to some authors, Cupid was the fruit of the love between Venus and Mars. Though the child was brought up with great care, he did not grow as other children did and remained pink, dimpled, small, and mischievous. Venus,

Venus and Eros.

concerned for her son, decided to consult Themis, who replied mysteriously "love cannot grow without passion". The attempts of the goddess to understand the hidden meaning behind Themis' reply were in vain, and it was not until *Antheros*, the god of passion, was born that Cupid grew into a handsome youth. But when the two separated, Cupid returned to his childlike appearance and mischievous games.

The Romans represented Venus as either totally naked or wearing a short dress called a *Cetus*, and she is probably the most recreated image of all the gods. There are several famous statues of her that stand in art galleries, but the most famous of all is the "Venus de Milo". The festivals celebrated in her honour were characterised by their elegant traditions, and her devotees wore garlands of fresh flowers, the emblem of natural beauty. The Romans dedicated the month of April to the goddess, as the month when nature represents the renewal of love.

The myth of Adonis in Rome

The Roman version of the myth of Adonis tells how Venus fell deeply in love with a young and daring hunter. The goddess made several vain attempts to persuade the youth to forget the pleasures of hunting in her arms, but the hunter left her each time to return to his hunting friends. One day, he came across a wild boar and attacked it bravely, but the injured animal turned on Adonis. He tried to get out of its way, but he was not quick enough, and the wild animal sank its powerful tusks into Adonis' side and killed him. The inconsolable goddess cried and cried for the death of her lover and her tears, as they touched the ground turned into anemones, and the drops of blood from Adonis' wounds stained the white roses red.

Mercury arrived, unwillingly, to transport the soul of the youth to the Underworld, where it was received with joy by Persephone. But Venus, unable to overcome her grief at the separation, implored Jupiter to free Adonis from death's embrace or she herself would accompany him into the Underworld.

Jupiter could not allow Beauty and Love to abandon the Earth, so he returned Adonis to life. But Persephone opposed his decision, having fallen for the beauty of the young man herself. After much argument, it was decided that Adonis would spend six months of the year with Persephone and six months with Venus. At the beginning of spring, Adonis left the Underworld, and on his return to the Earth, the flowers sprouted and the birds sang in joy. When he returned to the dark and cold reign of Pluto at the end of the summer, the crude winter, like the tusks of the boar, pierced his side, and the world lamented once again at his departure.

Analysis of the myth of Adonis in Rome

Some mythologists have uncovered a solar myth in this legend. According to their studies, Adonis was the short-lived Sun, killed by the boar, which represents the demon of darkness, and returned to life by the passion of the dawn, Venus, who was unable to live without him.

> *Mars in his armour will sit on the alter,*
> *Completely bathed in blood.*

Shakespeare

4. ARES, THE GOD OF WAR

Ares is the prince of war, a lover of battles purely for the pleasure of the fight; his sister *Eris*, meanwhile, creates causes for going to war. Ares had a brutal appearance and violent nature, which he unleashed with the killing of humans and the pillaging of cities, leading to his unpopularity amongst the other immortals, with the exceptions of Aphrodite, who fell madly in love with him, his sister Eris, and the greedy Hades, whom he provided with dead warriors from his merciless battles. But Ares also represented the force of passion and sensuality. In addition to his adulterous affair with Aphrodite, he is also named by some authors as the father of the Amazons.

The two sons Aphrodite bore him always accompanied him into battle: *Deimos* was the personification of terror, and his brother *Phobos* personified dread. Phobos whispered cowardice into the hearts of soldiers and urged them to flee.

Far from being an invincible god, Ares was defeated and humiliated by the cunning, calculating Athena in the Trojan War, and on another occasion, the giant sons of Aloeos conquered him and kept him prisoner in a bronze vase for years, until he was released by Hermes. Hercules also shot him in the thigh with an arrow, and the hero Diomedes forced him to flee, wounded and screaming, to the safety of Olympus.

On one occasion, he was accused by Poseidon of murdering his son Halirrhothius. Ares declared in his defence that the act had been totally justified, alleging that he had saved his own daughter Alcippe from being raped by him. With the absence of witnesses, the court declared him not guilty. This was the first verdict ever given for murder in the courts, and the hill where the incident had taken place was called Areopagus.

Analysis of Ares

Ares, the Thracian god, came from the generation of the twelve great gods of Olympus. However, he was the least important and the least worshipped in Greek culture, due to the pacific spirit of the Greek people, which contrasted with the god's character and attributes.

It is easy to understand why the Greeks, who were more inclined to respect the subtleties of reason and intelligence, bore a certain revulsion for the god who was to them a stranger both in temperament and origin. For this reason he is often represented in legends in battles from which he emerged defeated. In Rome, however, he was a highly esteemed god and was often confused with their own god Mars.

MARS, THE FEARSOME WARRIOR

The Roman god of war, unlike his Greek counterpart Ares, was one of the most important deities of the empire. It is said the god was born in Thrace, a region well-known for its warrior people and ferocious storms. Ares, who personified the angry sky covered by storm clouds, never had enough blood and fighting, preferring the clamour of battle over any music or tune. Nobody expected any honourable act from him, nor did they devote any prayers to him. On the contrary, he was a feared god, and people cowered in terror at the mention of his name. The Emperor Augustus ordered a temple to be built in his honour, which was given the name *Ultor*, meaning 'avenger'.

The god was also assimilated with *Quirinus*, the ancient Sabine god who personified war. Although in very ancient times, Quirinus carried out the mainly pacific role of protecting the farmers. Perhaps it was due to this influence that Mars, a destructive god by nature, was also considered the protector of vegetation, who ensured its natural cycle. He was also dedicated the month of flowers, March, when the first buds and blossoms of spring appear. Contemporary mythologists have tried to find a plausible explanation for the two opposing attributes of war and prosperity. They have demonstrated that the festivities held in his honour were celebrated at the beginning of the spring, at the time when armies came out after the winter's rest and went back to combat. Seen in another way, Mars would come to symbolise the awakening of the strength and vigour in both nature and the hearts of soldiers.

Mars is therefore a contradictory god, also demonstrated by the numerous interpretations made of him. The influence of the Greek god Ares does not conceal the fact that the primitive god has a more complex character and was especially worshipped by the Sabines and the Oscans, an Italian warrior people. However, the Romans knew him as the father of the founders of the city of Rome.

The legend of Romulus and Remus

King Procas of Alba Longa, descendant of the Trojan hero Aeneas, left two sons: Numitor, the elder and the legitimate heir to the throne, and Amulius. The younger son was much more ambitious and unscrupulous than his brother. His wickedness led him to imprison Numitor, kill his nephew Lausus in a hunting party, and commit his niece Ilia, or *Rhea Silvia,* to the consecrated order of the goddess Vesta, in order to take the throne for himself and remove all possible threat to his accession.

As a priestess of Vesta, Rhea Silvia was bound to remain a virgin and could not bear any heirs to the throne. However, Mars took a liking to her and continued to pester the young woman until she gave in to his desires. Twins were born from their union: *Romulus* and *Remus*. Amulius ordered his niece's execution for having broken her vows of chastity and abandoned the twins to fate in a basket on the River Tiber. But river's current carried the basket to the foot of a hill, where the city of Rome was to be founded years later. There, they were discovered by a she-wolf who had lost her cubs, and she gave the twins her milk. The twins later were adopted by shepherds, Faustulus and Acca Larentia, who brought them up and educated them. The twins grew up to be strong and bold and made a living from pillage.

On one occasion, Remus stole from Amulius' flock and was caught and imprisoned. Romulus then killed the usurper king and freed his brother, putting Numitor back on the throne. After leaving Alba, the twins decided to found a city on the shores of the River Tiber, in the spot where the river had left them as babiés, as thanks for not drowning them. However, their brotherly love was broken as soon as they came to discuss the name of the city and the limits they would establish for it. To put an end to the arguments, Romulus traced an imaginary wall as the limits of the city and forbade his brother to cross it. Remus laughed at him and his wall and jumped over the line. Romulus was furious for this sacrilegious act and killed his brother, but he later repented for his uncontrolled behaviour and buried Remus with full honours in the Aventine.

Venus and Mars.

Romulus was now the sole lord of Rome, and he gathered other adventurers as wild and uncontrolled as him, bandits from the nearby lands and even escaped slaves. But the leader of this tribe of ruffians realised that without a single woman in his city, the population would never grow. So he came up with a plan and announced to the entire region that games were to be celebrated in Rome to honour Consus, the god of the Underworld. He invited all the neighbouring Sabines, and while the celebrations were going on, Romulus' men kidnapped all the Sabine women. Their fathers took up arms against the kidnappers and the fighting was set to become fierce, but the Sabine women stood between their fathers and their new husbands and held up their children in protest at the fighting.

There are several versions of the tale of Romulus' death. One tells how he became a merciless king, and the senators, tired of his orders, took advantage of a solar eclipse to kill him, and cut him up, hiding the pieces of his body under their togas. When the light of day returned, and the people asked where their king was, the senators explained that the immortal gods had taken him to share their dignity and home, and from that day on, he should be worshipped as a true god, by the name of Quirinus. They also ordered that a temple be built in his honour on one of the seven hills, which was known as the Quirinal Hill, and the annual festivities in Rome celebrated in his honour were called the Quirinalia. Another legend, much more glorious, tells how after thirty years of wise reign, Romulus was ascended to the sky by his father Mars, in a violent storm.

Analysis of the legend

It is difficult and risky to consider Romulus as a real person in Roman history, as he almost certainly only existed in the legends of the ancient society. However, he must be recognised as a legendary character that justifies and divines the foundation of a city destined to dominate, for centuries, the world of the Mediterranean. In the same way, the legend of the kidnapping of the Sabine women alludes to the violent fusion of societies that went into the founding of Rome.

* * *

Mars was so satisfied with the new city of Rome, with its unruly and violent inhabitants, that he put it under his special protection. To communicate the news, he threw down a shield, called the 'Ancile', while the people of the city were praying, and they clearly heard his voice declaring that Rome would always survive whilst he was able to protect it. The Romans were delighted and placed the ceremonial shield in one of their main temples. But they soon started to fear that one of their enemies would steal it, and the people made eleven more shields in the exact image of the celestial Ancile, which only the guardian priests who were in constant watch over the shield were able to distinguish.

In March, the Anciles were displayed in processions that marched through the city, while the priests danced an invocation to Mars, banging the shields and chanting vulgar war songs. The month of March was dedicated to the god for its tempestuous weather.

Mars was generally represented wearing shining amour, with a plumed helmet on his proud head, a swinging lance in one hand, and a shield gripped firmly in the other, in a warrior stance ready to confront his enemies.

His assistants, or his sons, according to some authors, were Eris, the personification of discord; Phobos, alarm; Metus, fear; Deimos, dread; and Pallor, terror. Bellona, or Nerio, a Sabine divinity, often accompanied him, armed with a lance and carrying a helmet. He drove the god's chariot, steering through dangerous attacks and occupying himself with the god's safe passage. Bellona was often confused with the Greek god Enyo, Ares' messenger, who was a lover of blood and slaughter. On the battlefields she enjoyed hearing war cries, the screams of pain, and the whimpering of the injured. Mars and Bellona were worshipped in the same temples, and their altars were the only ones stained with the blood of human sacrifices.

Those who worshipped Mars were mainly young Romans and soldiers, and their field of action was called Mars' Field or the Martian Field in his honour. The crowns of laurel leaves that were given to the victorious Generals after a battle were left at the feet of the warrior god's statue, and a bull was offered in sacrifice as thanks for a successful campaign.

> *Then the gods left for their heavenly vault,*
> *The shining monuments of Vulcan art.*
> *Jupiter reclined his stately head on his divan,*
> *While Juno slept on a golden bed.*

> Homer

5. HEPHAESTUS, THE GOD OF THE FORGE

It is said that when Hera gave birth to Hephaestus and saw his ugliness and frailty, she was horrified and disgusted at having borne such a child, and hurled the baby from the peak of Olympus to rid herself of the shame. Fortunately, the baby fell into the sea and was rescued by Tethys and Eurynome, who were close by. The two gods brought the child up in an underground grotto, where Hephaestus installed his first iron forge. In thanks to Tethys, who always took care of him, he forged weapons for her son Achilles.

After nine years, Hera began to notice that Tethys was wearing particularly beautiful jewels, and, curious, she asked her where she had got them. Tethys hesitated at first, but in the end she told Hera the truth about Hephaestus. Ashamed and full of regret, Hera went to find her son and took him back to Olympus, where she gave him a much better forge than his previous one. Some say that it was she who solved his marital problems with Aphrodite.

Hephaestus was soon able to forgive Hera, and he even dared to criticise Zeus when he punished and humiliated his wife by hanging her by the wrists from the sky for rebelling against him. Zeus, furious at this lack of respect, took Hephaestus in his powerful grip and threw him with such force that he landed on the island of Lemnos, breaking both legs. After that unlucky day, he could only walk with the help of crutches, which he forged himself from gold.

A second theory about Hephaestus' birth is that Hera created him out of jealousy after Zeus created his daughter Athena alone. Zeus did not believe her, and he put her in a mechanical chair with arms that folded across the seat and forced her to swear on the River Styx that she was telling the truth.

Hephaestus is the god of fire and, thus, of civilisation. He was the creator of fire, which he gave to the world of humans through Prometheus. The divine smith came from the East and is the forger of weapons, the creator of the golden palaces of the gods, and the maker of utensils and devices that helped him in his ever-active forge. His physical defects made him a passive god, and he was loved by the other gods and mortals alike. He is considered the patron of artisans, who instils them with the creative force when at their artistic labour.

Analysis of the god Hephaestus

Hephaestus is the most demystified of the gods, perhaps because his activities were so much more normal than the other deities. He represented social progress and technology and came to be considered the god of civilisation – brought to Earth by Prometheus through fire. He was the only god that worked and was the patron of artisans. He spent his time in his underground forge, where he forged beautiful creations with his hammer and anvil. It is interesting that the ugliest of the gods created such beautiful things.

The story of his birth and how his mother reacted to his ugliness by hurling him from the mountain was taken up as a tradition of the Spartans. Babies that did not pass 'the test' ended up as vulture food at the bottom of a cliff.

VULCAN, THE GOD OF FIRE

Vulcan came from distant lands, probably Etruscan, but he lost his indigenous characteristics, as did all the primitive gods, when the Greek gods invaded the Roman pantheon. At first, he was worshipped as a great god, as the god of fire, the primordial element in human evolution and technological progress. Later, when he came to be assimilated with Hephaestus, he was reduced to the simple god of the forge, who forged and worked the weapons of the gods in the caverns of volcanoes in southern Italy.

Vulcan did not live on Olympus for more than a brief period, from when his mother Juno accepted him as her son to when Jupiter hurled him to earth. From then on, it was unusual to see him at the councils of the gods on Olympus. He lived in the depths of a mountain called Etna, where he found a great fire that he used to install his forge. The Cyclops helped him there to forge useful objects and tools with the metals that he mined from the heart of the mountain. Amongst these objects were two machines made of gold in the shape of women, which worked for him as servants. This legend gave rise to the word 'robot'.

Mount Etna, whose peak towered above the city of Catania, also served as the prison for Typhon and Enceladus, the rebellious giants who were defeated by the gods of Olympus. Some legends tell us that the smoke and fire that escaped from the crater of the mountain came from the fiery breath of the imprisoned giants. According to the Greek legend, the volcano was given the name of a nymph, daughter of Uranus and Gaea, who acted as referee between Demeter and Hephaestus in the fight over the island of Sicily. Roman mythology tells that it was the home of Vulcan and his assistants, where the armour of the gods and heroes was forged, and this was the reason for the smoke and fire that spouted from the mouth of the volcano.

In addition to wedding Venus, Vulcan also married one of the Graces, but she soon became bored with the god and left him, as Venus also did. Vulcan's sons were mostly monsters, such as Cacus, Periphetes, and Cercion, who had

Mars, Venus and Vulcan.

important roles in heroic mythology. Vulcan was worshipped by smiths and artisans, who recognised him as their special patron and celebrated great festivals – the Vulcanalia and the Hephaestia – in his honour.

Analysis of the god Vulcan

The Romans considered Vulcan the god of dangerous and destructive fire, who created the volcano Etna in a temper. In this way, they explained the strange and dangerous behaviour of the mountain. The word 'volcano' comes directly from the name of the Roman god, and volcanism, in geological terms, is the process that results in the formation of volcanoes and lava.

> *Jupiter took it from his stately head,*
> *Adorned in war armour,*
> *Golden and bright.*

> Shelley

6. ATHENA, THE WISE WARRIOR

Athena's birth is one of the most amazing, not just in the way she was born, but also because, apart from various monsters, she was the only deity to be born an adult. Her priestesses told of Zeus' desire for a sexual relationship with Metis (Wisdom), the Titan. She tried to escape from him by taking on different shapes, but Zeus was cunning and pursued her until he caught her by surprise and left her pregnant. Gaea, the Mother Earth, declared from her oracle that she would bear a girl, but if Metis conceived again, it would be a boy who would become more powerful then Zeus himself and, following tradition, would dethrone him. In fear, Zeus persuaded Metis to repose in her bed, where he swallowed her whole. Afterwards he said that she would advise him from inside his stomach.

One day, while he walked along the shore of Lake Triton,

Zeus felt a terrible pain in his head. He thought it was about to explode and started to scream in fright, until the vaults of heaven resounded with the echo of his terror. Hermes rushed to his aid and soon realised the cause of Zeus' pain. He told Hephaestus to bring his vice and tools, to open Zeus' skull. From his head sprang Athena with a terrible war cry, adult and fully armed.

Athena was the goddess of war and wisdom, a trait she inherited from her mother. She invented the flute, the trumpet, the clay pot, the plough, the rake, the cart, and the ship. She was the first to teach science, numbers, and all the arts of women. Though the goddess of war, she was a peaceful goddess, preferring to resolve disputes and maintain the law with pacific methods. Unlike Ares, she took no pleasure from battle. Normally, in times of peace, she carried no weapon, but she is often represented armed with a breast-plate, a shield, a golden lance, and the coat of arms depicting the head of Medusa. In other representations, she appears with the winged symbol of victory in her left hand.

Athena was the goddess who enjoyed the most prestige in Olympus, after Zeus and Hera. This preference by the Greek people is demonstrated by one of their most relevant myths, in the dispute that she had with Poseidon concerning the spiritual possession of the region of Attica. In one version of the fight to obtain the region, Poseidon demonstrated his power by driving his trident into a rock from which salt water flowed to form a beautiful lake or, in other versions, a beautiful and swift horse. Athena, however, offered an olive branch to the Greek people, symbol of peace and wealth. The people judged that the olive branch would be more advantageous and chose her as their protector. To commemorate her victory over Poseidon, Athena gave her own name to the city, Athens, and taught its people to honour her as their goddess. Thus Athena became the protector of the state, guaranteeing just laws and their application in the courts and assemblies. The goddess also protected each family, as she stood for the understanding and chastity of spouses, the honour of the home and the health of all. She was also known as Athena Hygiea.

Like Hestia and Artemis, Athena retained her virginity, despite receiving several proposals from various gods, Titans, and giants. It is said she rejected them all and was never attracted by any.

* * *

Athena was as modest and pure as Artemis, but still more generous. One day, Tyresias surprised her accidentally when she was bathing, and Athena put her hands over his eyes and made him blind. But she gave him the gift of internal sight as compensation.

Analysis of the goddess Athena

The goddess was endowed with high intelligence and, thanks to her mother, a contemplative character. She became a valued advisor to the other gods, particularly helping them to defeat the giants.

During the course of the Trojan War, the goddess protected the great heroes of Attica and most of the Greek chiefs. Her attributions rapidly increased, and she was soon not just the chaste goddess who blinded Tyresias for seeing her naked and the armoured goddess of war, but the protector of the entire state, the goddess who assured the justice of the laws and the courts. She also showed a particular interest in agriculture and was the inventor of the plough. Thanks to her happy influence of reason and her reflexive and subtle manner, Athena provided an extended and constant spiritual energy to the arts and literature.

The goddess was thus the divine symbol of Greek civilisation, and her warrior's strength, intelligence, wisdom, and modesty gave her the power to carry out her dominion over the world. The story of the dispute between Athena and Poseidon for the possession of Attica has an interpretation that explains the absence of women in political life. It claims that the men of the region voted in favour of Poseidon and the women for Athena, winning by a single vote. Angry at the result, Poseidon unleashed his powers over the

Athena.

sea and flooded the region. In order to pacify him, the people were forced to take away the women's right to vote.

MINERVA, THE GODDESS OF WISDOM

Minerva originates from ancient Etrusca and became so important to Roman mythology that she formed part of the captioning triad with Jupiter and Juno. She represented intelligent thinking, art and literature, music, and intellect and wisdom – all allegorical images found in abundance in Roman religion. With the arrival of Greek culture, Minerva and Athena came to be worshipped as the same figure, and it is almost impossible to distinguish her Roman characteristics from those she had in Greece.

When Minerva was born out of Jupiter's head, she became a member of the deity family and had the responsibilities of presiding over peace and defensive warfare. She also represented the incarnation of wisdom and substituted the goddess Stupidity, who had governed over the world until then and who was the daughter of Chaos and Eternal Night.

Minerva was always at her father Jupiter's side offering him advice. In wartime, she took up her shield, the Aegis, and went out to defend those whose cause she considered just. The goddess was wise and just and did not fear the battlefield, for she was never defeated. She compensated for her masculine tendencies for battle with a love of sewing, and she was said to be as skilful with a needle as she was with a sword.

Minerva had numerous and majestic temples and altars dedicated to her, as well as many beautiful statues sculpted in her image by great artists. The most well-known was created by Phydias and measured forty feet in height, showing the image of a beautiful woman in battle dress, armed from head to toe, with a lance and a shield in her hands.

In Greece, festivals were held in her honour, such as the Panathena, which was celebrated every four years. In Rome, however, there were annual festivities such as the Minervalia or Quincuatrus. In these festivals, the statue of the goddess that was believed to have fallen from the skies was carried in procession through the entire city while the spectators sang and shouted her praise.

> *What can afflict her that she does not return home?*
> *Demeter searches for her everywhere,*
> *With a permanent frown of worry on her forehead*
> *From morning to nightfall,*
> *"My life, though immortal, is nothing!"*
> *She cries, "In your absence, Persephone! Perse-*
> *phone!"*

Ingellow

7. DEMETER, THE GODDESS OF FERTILITY

Demeter, the daughter of Cronus and Gaea and the sister of Zeus, is the goddess of the wheat fields, protecting them and ensuring the growth of the crops. For this reason, in all the lands of Ancient Greece, where the economy was largely based on the cultivation of grains, there are many local legends about the goddess. She came from the third generation of gods and became the new Mother Earth, though more accessible and humanised. She also personified fertility and agricultural richness, and was considered the inventor of the grain harvest. Demeter is the antithesis of Hera, mother rather than wife, with a generous and peaceful spirit, capable of giving her life for her children.

At the weddings of Cadmus and Harmony, Demeter fell in love with the Titan *Iasion*. They slipped away from the festivities and made love in a field that had been worked three times. Zeus noticed her absence and was enraged to find her with Iasion in the middle of a field. He struck Iasion down with lightning. Months later, in Crete, the goddess bore a son, Pluto, who took up a place between Fertility and Abundance in the Greek pantheon.

Poseidon once tried to seduce Demeter, but she was not interested in him. She transformed herself into a mare to

85

escape from him, but Poseidon took the form of an amorous stallion and mated with her. From this scandalous encounter, the nymph Despoina and the steed Arion were born. But Demeter is best known for her part in the legend of the kidnapping of her daughter Persephone, or Kore.

The kidnapping of Persephone

When Demeter was young, she was seduced by her brother Zeus, and they had two children: the luxurious Iacchos and the sweet and lovely Kore, whom Demeter adored. Hades fell in love with Kore and asked Zeus' permission to marry her. Zeus knew Demeter would refuse, but he did not want to offend his brother, and he replied that he could neither give his permission, nor refuse it. Hades took the answer as his consent.

One day, Kore was playing with friends in Attica, on the plains of Eleusis, where they were gathering flowers. Suddenly she saw a beautiful narcissus. She was about to pick it when the Earth opened and her uncle, Hades, appeared. He picked her up, and though she screamed and struggled, he carried her away. Her screams reached the ears of Demeter, who left Olympus to search for her. She wandered without rest, her way lit by a torch, for nine days and nights, neither eating, nor drinking, nor washing. She asked everybody, but none knew anything of her daughter's mysterious disappearance. Only the old Hecate said she had heard Kore's voice shouting "Kidnap! Kidnap!" But when she had run to help, there had been no sign of the girl.

On the tenth day, Demeter asked Celeus and Metaneira, the king and queen of Eleusis, for help. They took her in very respectfully, and in appreciation for their hospitality, the goddess decided to grant their small son, Demophon, the gift of immortality. As part of the necessary magical ritual, Demeter had to hold the child over flames to burn his mortality, but Metaneira entered the room in the middle of the ritual and broke the spell, and the child died. To console the parents, Demeter taught their other son, Triptolemus, the art of cultivating the fields, sowing the land, and harvesting grains.

Demeter and Kore.

However, since Demeter had left Olympus, the land had become sterile, and hunger and misery were threatening the Earth. Zeus sent a message through Iris that she leave the search and return to Olympus. Demeter refused to go back without her daughter, and she went with Hecate to speak Helios, who sees all. She forced him to admit that Hades had been the kidnapper. Demeter was so furious that she continued to wander around the world preventing the trees from giving fruit and the grass from growing.

Zeus, in desperation, realised he only had one choice, so he begged Hades to return Kore before the Earth dried up completely. However, the god of the Underworld refused, saying that during her stay in the world of the dead, the girl had eaten a pomegranate, which meant she could never return to the world of the living. Finally they reached an agreement. Kore would spend six months with her mother and six months with her husband Hades, as queen of Tartarus and with the name Persephone.

Analysis of the legend

The symbolism of this etiological legend is as beautiful as it is easy to interpret, for it explains the phenomena and procedures related to the cultivation of the land and, particularly, for fruit that has periods of production, ripening and absence.

Demeter, which means god-mother, was the goddess of agriculture and fertility and the mother of Kore, which means maiden in Ancient Greek, who symbolises the grains of cereal.

Before sprouting, the grain is buried in the earth, symbolised by the kidnapping of Kore. In her absence, which is the winter, fertility, represented by Demeter, abandons humanity, and the lands are sterile, and the leaves dry and fall off the trees, and their fruits disappear.

This period could also coincide with a period of hunger that struck Greece. The people begged Zeus to intervene. After reaching an agreement, Kore, now Persephone, is found by her mother in Eleusis, where from then on an important fertility ritual in honour of Demeter was celebrated. This is the return of the spring, which causes the germination of seeds, and the flowers and fruits appear again.

The fertility rituals of Eleusis were held in October. Like the harvest festivities they were reserved for married women only. The cult evolved toward a more profound significance, related to the cycle of life and death: earth-grain-human-earth. A cycle in which nothing dies, everything is reborn through the Earth and is transformed, this rebirth later was to be understood as the transmigration of the soul, which returns to the Earth to continue its journey of ultimate purification.

Some mythologists believe the myth of Adonis is a version of the myth of Persephone. They see in both the personification of the crops, visibly prospering during the six warmer months and remaining dormant under the cold earth for the rest of the year.

The legend of Triptolemus would explain the birth of agriculture. However, the Greeks first thought this came from the Nile Valley, in Egypt, and had been invented by the Egyptian god Isis, whose most important work was the invention of the cultivation of cereals. The cultivation of vines, however, was a gift from the god Osiris. The Greeks later identified Isis with Demeter and Osiris with Dionysus and claimed it was Demeter who had given the first grains of wheat to Celeus, the first king of Eleusis, and taught the labour of the land to Buciges, who put oxen to the plough, and taught Triptolemus to sow seeds, to whom she gave a cart pulled by two dragons.

On some occasions, Triptolemus was associated with Demeter and Persephone in a type of trinity of fertility. It has also been said that it was he who introduced the mysteries of Eleusis and established the cult of Demeter in the city.

* * *

Erysichthon, the son of King Triopas of Thessaly, was one of the few men whom Demeter had to treat harshly. Erysichthon invaded the goddess' sacred orchard and cut down the trees there to build a banquet hall. To persuade him to stop, Demeter adopted the form of Nycippe, the priestess

89

of the orchard, but instead of obeying her, Erysichthon threatened her with his axe. Then the goddess changed back to her real form and condemned him to suffer eternal hunger. The more he ate, the hungrier and thinner he became, until his parents could no longer allow themselves the luxury of providing him more food, and he had to become a beggar, wandering through the streets eating rubbish. It was even said that his daughter Mestra sold herself as a slave for her love for him, to provide him with food for a while.

Analysis of the goddess Demeter

Demeter was a goddess, but above all she was a mother. When she conceived Persephone, who symbolises grain, she took on the double role of the mother who gives birth to a child and the earth that nourishes the seed. She is the model for Greek women, responsible for both the first education of her children and the cultivation of the land. In ancient times, while the men dedicated their time to fishing, hunting, or weapons, the women looked after the home and the fields. This might explain why it was a goddess and not a god who protected the harvests.

As the goddess of fertility and the harvest, she settled the nomadic peoples, taught them to organise a community, harness their animals, sow and plough, gather the harvest, and store and grind the grain to make flour. The myth of Demeter condenses the history of migration and settlement. Through the centuries, Demeter's attributions multiplied. She was honoured by the peoples initiated into the mysteries as one of the main divinities of abundance and fertility, as well as by farmers, who celebrated festivals such as the Thesmophoriazusae and the Eleusinia at harvest time.

CERES, THE GODDESS OF AGRICULTURE

Before becoming linked with the goddess Demeter, *Ceres* was an ancient Roman goddess. Her name comes

Demeter.

from the verb *crescere*, to grow, which indicates the attributes of the goddess – she was the life that came from the land. Ceres formed a part of the Estonian gods, she gave life to the young and fragile shoots, ripened the wheat and turned the harvest golden.

For the Romans, Ceres was the goddess of agriculture and civilisation, and her daughter *Proserpine*, born from her relationship with Jupiter, was the goddess of plants. This goddess was soon assimilated with Persephone, who became Pluto's wife and queen of the Underworld, but who extended her special protection to the germination of seeds.

The Romans said that Persephone's favourite places were in the beautiful meadows of Enna or the green fields of Mount Etna, on the island of Sicily. It was there that, according to Roman legend, she was kidnapped by Pluto. The rest of the legend only differed in small details such as that Ceres disguised herself as an old woman so as not to be recognised.

There also exists a small anecdote about the goddess that says how during her long journey searching for her lost daughter, a youth called Estelle offered her a plate of porridge. The goddess accepted it so quickly that the youth laughed at her. To punish the youth for his rudeness, she threw the rest of the porridge in his face and turned him into a lizard.

Ceres discovered the whereabouts of her daughter by throwing her sash into the Ciane and asking the water nymph to tell her mother what had happened. Although she knew where her daughter was, there was nothing she could do. She shut herself into a dark cave, where she cried inconsolably and ignored her responsibilities. The rain stopped refreshing the flowers, the grass perished, and the grain dried out under the sun's rays. The lands were struck with famine, but the goddess took no notice of the pleas or the desperate prayers of the hungry people and swore that nothing would grow on the earth while her daughter was in Pluto's kingdom. So the people turned their pleas to Jupiter, who had to involve himself in the matter. He negotiated Proserpine's release with his brother, and they reached an agreement by which she would leave the Underworld providing she had eaten no food there during her stay. Ceres was about to embrace her daughter when Aescalphos appeared, a guardian spirit who had seen Proserpine biting a pomegranate, then Jupiter decreed that for each grain that she had eaten she must pass a month of each year in her husband's terrible kingdom.

Ceres punished the excessive zeal of the guardian by turning him into an owl, and Proserpine was condemned to spend six months of each year with Pluto and six months with her beloved mother. Mercury was chosen to accompany her, and every time he took her from her cold and macabre prison, the skies cleared, the Sun shone, the grass grew afresh, and the flowers sprang from the land at her step, with the blessing of her mother. But when she left the Earth again, Ceres was so upset that the skies cried for her, and no flower or plant dared to blossom, and she returned to her cave until the day her daughter surfaced again.

As nature changed, so did Proserpine. When she was in the Underworld, she became pale and lifeless, and when she returned to the surface, she acquired her characteristic splendour and vitality.

There were many temples dedicated to Ceres and her daughter. In Italy, great annual festivals called the Thesmophoriazusae and the Cerealia were celebrated, and orchards were dedicated to them. Ceres was generally represented as a voluptuous woman, dressed in flowing robes and sometimes crowned with ears of wheat or holding either a sheaf of wheat or the horn of abundance.

> *To Poseidon, the powerful sea god, he sang;*
> *Mover of the Earth, and god of the fruitless ocean,*
> *Be blessed and with your observant hand*
> *Help those under your terrible domain.*

Homer

8. POSEIDON, THE GOD OF THE TRIDENT

When Zeus shared his kingdom with his two brothers, Poseidon received the wide oceans. For this reason, he was also known as the god of the Mediterranean. Other versions however, say that the three brothers drew lots for who would have control of what, leaving Earth as the property of all three. Poseidon, who was equal to his brother in dignity and bearing, though not in power, was naturally gloomy, argumentative, and ambitious. He desired possession of the realms of Earth, but he rarely came out the victor in any dispute. On separate occasions, he unsuccessfully fought with Helios for possession of the city of Corinth, Hera for Argos, and Athena for the region of Attica.

He built the magnificent underwater palace of Aegea, in Eubeia. In the spacious stables, he kept a team of white horses and a golden chariot, and when the chariot approached, any storm immediately ceased.

Poseidon also was considered the god of the horse. Perhaps this was due to the argument over the possession of Attica, when according to the legend, to convince the people that they should choose him and not Athena, he struck the ground, and a swift horse sprang forth. At times, he took the form of a horse in the pursuit of a goddess, such as Demeter. In some festivals and rites, horses were offered in his honour.

As his chosen wife would need to feel at home in the depths of the sea, Poseidon first courted the Nereid Tethys. But when Themis prophesised that any son borne by her would become more important than his father, he married a mortal woman called Peleus. Later he fell for *Amphitrite*, the daughter of Nereus and Doris. He had seen her one day while she was playing with her sisters the Nereids and wanted her straight away as his wife. But Amphitrite was not struck with the idea and escaped, seeking refuge as far away from the sea as possible, next to Atlas. Poseidon sent messengers, amongst them *Delphinus*, who presented the god's case with such charm that Amphitrite gave in. In thanks, Poseidon put the image of Delphinus amongst the stars in a constellation, the dolphin.

Amphitrite gave Poseidon three sons: *Triton*, *Rhode*, and *Benthesikyme*. Like Zeus, Poseidon cheated on his wife several times, though she never sought revenge, like Hera did. In fact, Poseidon was famous in Olympus for his affairs

Poseidon.

with immortal women and even with monsters, such as *Medusa*, with whom he had terrible offspring, such as the *Cercopes*, the *Alaodae*, *Chrysaor*, and the *Cyclops Polyphemus*, who died by the hand of the hero Ulysses.

Analysis of the god Poseidon

Far from being a revered god, Poseidon was feared by the people. Perhaps he earned his fame with the wicked beings that he created, the *Telchines*. His fury is shown by the merciless power of the oceans, and his violent demonstrations of rage are terrible to behold, for he is the god of the tremors that shake both the earth and the sea in his wild power.

According to legend, Poseidon left his home in a chariot drawn by horses the colour of seaweed and the foam of the sea, to direct the movement of the waves, pacify or create storms, striking the water with his trident or shouting orders in a deep powerful voice.

For a people that sailed a great deal, as the Greeks did, the god of the sea was a great lord, with whom it was important to maintain good relations. He was worshipped by sailors, who begged him to grant them a safe voyage, and the prayers and sacrifices offered to him were frequent and generous, held in coastal sanctuaries and in the middle of storms.

The god's power extended to fresh water and the nymph spirits of these waters. In dispelling the humidity in the air, he favoured the fertility of the land and often was considered an agricultural god.

The god reached Ancient Greece with the first migrations of the Indo-European peoples from central Europe, who first used the horse in Mediterranean culture. It is not unusual that he was considered the god of the horse, nor that the winged horse *Pegasus*, sired from his relations with Medusa, was his offspring. His wings, a symbol of progress, also appear on bulls in Syrian culture. However, if the horse was associated with Poseidon in remembrance of his primitive origins, once he became the god of the sea, he adopted the bull as his image, the symbol of the strength of the waters and fertility, common to Near Eastern cultures. From these roots also springs the myth that Poseidon sent King Minus of Crete a bull for sacrifice, which later sired the *Minotaur*.

NEPTUNE, THE LORD OF THE SEAS

In the primitive religions of the peoples of Lazio, Neptune was not considered the god of the sea, as these nations dedicated themselves to agriculture. Unlike the Roman people, the economy of the Greeks was based on maritime trading. Therefore, when Roman mythology absorbed the Greek legends and traditions, Neptune was identified with Poseidon and gradually lost his previous characteristics. Though in exchange, he received the new characteristics of his Greek counterpart and came to be accepted by the Romans as the god of humidity, the lord of all the waters on the face of the earth, and the sole monarch of the oceans. Neptune substituted *Oceanus*, who never looked kindly upon his usurper and considered him inadequate to govern the aquatic world. But Neptune was not satisfied with his kingdom, and his ambitious nature led him to challenge Minerva for sovereignty of Athens and Apollo for that of Corinth, both of which he lost. However, the other gods considered him the most powerful among them, excepting only Jupiter.

Still unsatisfied, Poseidon stood against Jupiter, supported by Juno and Apollo. As punishment, the all-powerful king of the gods condemned Poseidon and his son to a year of exile on the Earth, where they were put to work for Laomedon and for whom they built the great wall of Troy. The king promised them a generous reward for their labour, but once the wall was finished, the dishonest, greedy king refused to hand over a single coin. In vengeance, Apollo set a plague on his people, and Neptune created a terrible monster that devoured everything within its reach. From then on, Neptune and Apollo professed themselves enemies of the Trojans and stood with the Greeks in the famous war.

Like Pluto and Vulcan, Neptune did not live in Olympus and only went there to attend banquets or ceremonies or when called to an important meeting. He usually inhabited his coral palaces built around the Mediterranean, and his power was such that a single word from him would cause or calm the most furious storm or raise the waves in fury. His dominion extended over the seas, rivers, lakes, and streams, and he could create earthquakes at will.

One legend tells that Neptune was the father of the famous *Golden Fleece*. It tells how he fell in love with a beautiful lady called *Theophane*. Fearful that one of the many suitors who pursued her would woo her before he could, he turned her into a sheep and carried her to the island of Crumissa. There, he transformed himself into a ram and courted her, and the offspring from this union was a ram with a fleece of gold.

It is also told that Neptune was the father of the giants *Otos* and *Eficaltes*, as well as *Neleus*, *Pelias*, and *Polyphemus*, who he had with Medusa when she was a beautiful young woman. But his legitimate wife was Amphitrite, or Salacia, with whom he had Triton, half man, half fish. Neptune's entourage was formed by the Nereids; the tritons, descendants of his son; and other minor gods, such as Proteus, who was in charge of the flocks of the ocean depths. Proteus also possessed the gift of prophecy and the ability to transform himself into any shape, though he was very reluctant to make use of the former.

Neptune was represented by the Romans as a mature man with long flowing hair and beard, wearing a crown of seaweed and brandishing his trident. His main worshippers were sailors and horse trainers, and he had numerous temples in Italy. He was usually worshipped with his wife Amphitrite, represented as a beautiful naked nymph, crowned in seaweed and coral and reclining on a chariot made of a giant conch shell drawn by dolphins or sea horses. Other temples were dedicated solely to the worship of Neptune himself, where games were held in his honour, the most famous of which were the Isthmian Games, a national festival celebrated in Corinth, on the isthmus of the same name, every four years.

Neptune.

And the temple brings
The terrible Hestia, with all her sacred things,
Her stately robes and the fire
Of which the sacred flames never go out.

Virgil

9. HESTIA, THE VIRGIN GODDESS OF FIRE

Hestia, the daughter of Cronus and Rhea, came from the generation of the twelve great divinities of Olympus. She was the goddess of the hearth, protecting those who asked her in all homes and public establishments.

The goddess was universally respected, not only as she was the most tranquil, correct, and charitable of the Olympian gods, but also because she had invented the art of building houses, and her fire was so sacred that if it was ever allowed to go out, whether by accident or as a sign of mourning, the flames were coaxed back to life by a lighting wheel.

Hestia, like Artemis and Athena, always resisted the amorous offers that she received, for after the destruction of Cronus, when Poseidon and Apollo offered themselves as rival suitors, she swore on the head of Zeus that she would remain a virgin forever. Zeus, to show his thanks for preserving the peace in Olympus, granted her the first victim of all public sacrifices made.

It is believed that her origins were Greek or Indo-European, and she symbolises purity through fire. Her mythology is almost non-existent, though she had an important cult in Rome.

Analysis of the goddess Hestia

Given the lack of legends and myths about Hestia, there is not much to add. Her significance rests on the fact that she was considered the protector of the family, the city, and the colonies. When the Greeks founded a new colony, they carried Hestia's sacred flame with them, destined to light the hearth of the new patria.

Hestia was unalterable and immutable, symbolising religious permanence, the continuity of civilisation and its light, in spite of emigration, destruction, revolution, and the various vicissitudes of the times. Some legends tell that she ceded her place in Olympus to Dionysus, the last Olympian god.

VESTA, THE GODDESS OF THE HEARTH

Vesta was one of the great Roman deities, much more important than Hestia in Greece, with whom she was later combined. Her cult, established in far remote times, worshipped her above all as the goddess of the home. Unlike the other gods, she was not represented as a statue in human form, but as fire, her living symbol. She was the goddess of fire and the family hearth, guardian spirit of humanity. She was worshipped principally in Italy, though she also had temples in Asia Minor and Greece.

Each city in Italy had its own hearth and sacred fire. The fire was guarded by the goddesses' priestesses, the *Vestals*, a highly respected feminine congregation who made a vow of chastity, as their goddess had done. The girls were selected from amongst the daughters of the patriarchal families by the Pontifice Maximus, the head of state religion, when they were six or seven years old. They lived in a building close to the circular temple of Vesta, which was located in the forum. Their stay there lasted thirty years and was divided into sections: the first decade was dedicated to their training, the second to their duties to the cult, and the third as instructors. The *Vestal Virgins*, as they were known, were those charged with the conservation of the sacred flame, the symbol of the state's prosperity. Their training was very strict, and punishment for the failure to fulfil any duty, especially that of chastity, was severe. They were condemned to be buried alive in a vaulted chamber, constructed solely for this purpose by the second king of Rome, Numa Pompilius.

The Vestals were so vigilant and pure that, in a thousand years, only eighteen failed to comply with all their duties. Once their thirty years was up, the women were free to stay at the temple or to leave and marry, if they so desired, and they were always treated with deep respect, regardless of the path they chose to follow. In exchange for their thirty years of devotion at the service of the state, they received certain privileges, such as occupying the seat of honour at public ceremonies and festivities or the power to pardon criminals who were lucky enough to cross her path on their way to the place of execution.

The most beautiful and noble girls who were given the privilege of becoming Vestal Virgins were dressed in pure white linen, with purple trimming and a purple cloak. At festivals, the Vestals, who were amongst the most popular and splendid women in Rome, wore their best robes and carried the sacred flame, attended by their Roman matrons, who went barefoot singing the praises of the great goddess.

In times of war, the vestals took the sacred flame to a safe place. On several occasions, it was taken out of Rome and transported on the Tiber, so that it would not fall into enemy hands. The Romans believed that the cult of the virtuous goddess had been introduced by Aeneas, who had selected the first Vestal, according to the legend. The virgin priestesses continued under his charge until the reign of Theodosius the Great, who converted to Christianity in the year 380 and abolished the cult, extinguished the sacred flame, and broke up the order of the Vestals.

Analysis of the goddess Vesta

In order to understand the importance and significance of Vesta within Roman religion, we should know that, in those times, the family hearth had a very different meaning from that of today, as it was considered the family alter. The head of the family would offer daily prayers and sacrifices in front of the hearth. The ancient Romans believed that the sacred fire had been sparked by the rays of the sun, and that if it was ever allowed to go out, it would mean the disgrace of all Rome. The sacred fire was guarded in the temple of Vesta, a beautiful circular temple where the Palladium of Troy was supposedly kept.

Moreover, the sacred flame was the emblem of the flame of life, which was believed to be kept alight in each human breast by Vesta, the life-giver. The sacred flame was maintained constantly alight and was never allowed to die. It also represented the purity and virginity of the goddess.

> *Her decrees*
> *To the guilty soul imposed the burning doors*
> *Of Tartarus, or sent the good*
> *To live in peace and eternal health*
> *In the Elysian Fields.*

> Akenside

10. HADES, THE GOD OF THE DEAD

After the universe was divided into three parts, Hades converted himself into the king of the Underworld. In some shadowy part of the kingdom, perhaps close to the River Erebus, the darkest part of all, was his palace, where he lived with his wife Persephone and to which nobody else had access.

Hades was a barbarous and feared god, though just. He did not represent death; he was simply the god of the dead. His duties kept him so occupied that he rarely left his kingdom to go to Olympus, and maybe for this reason he was not usually included in the list of Olympian gods. Hades only visited the Earth for work matters, or when he felt a desire for luxury. Persephone was faithful to her husband, though they had no children, for she preferred the company of Hecate, the goddess of witches, to that of her husband. Faced with this abandonment, Hades had numerous passing affairs with mortals or the nymphs of plants and the woods. Persephone was the cruel goddess of the Underworld during six months of the year, and she became sweet and compassionate during her other six months on earth.

Hades was feared by the Greeks and was an implacable force of justice, who sat in the depths of the Underworld with a sceptre in his hand and governed the souls of the dead who inhabited his unknown and shadowy realm without pity. Hades owned the helmet of invisibility, given to him by the Cyclops, which was his most prized possession. On occasions he lent it to the legendary heroes whom he had decided to help. All the riches of jewels and precious metals below the earth belonged to him, but he had no property in the world above.

The god lived surrounded by the infernal deities, his servants and his messengers, and he dictated the terrible law of death to the Earth. Hades was also called Pluto by the Romans, the distributor of wealth, and was invoked by farmers, to whom he represented a placid god who held the horn of abundance in one hand and ploughing tools in the other.

Tartarus and the Underworld

In *The Iliad*, Tartarus is the place furthest beneath the Earth, at the bottom of the Underworld and separated from the surface of the Earth by the same distance that separates the Earth from the sky. Tartarus was a dark, impenetrable abyss, surrounded by a triple wall made of bronze. It was where Cronus threw his children and where the Titans and giants defeated by Zeus were exiled, as well as all the divinities who infringed the laws of Olympus.

Tartarus is at the bottom of all things, beyond which there is nothing. The Roman poets called it the *Inferno*, an insufferable place in the depths of an abyss, where the guilty were sent as eternal punishment.

It was also said that Inferno was the place where the souls of humans went after death, but over the centuries the idea of the Inferno has evolved according to the philosophical doctrines concerning the immortality of the soul, punishment and the rewards offered by the lands beyond life. The descriptions made of the Inferno gradually became more numerous and more precise, and finally came to be separated into the places where good souls were rewarded and sinners punished.

> *The descent of Avernus is easy:*
> *The black door of Pluto is open day and night;*
> *What is difficult is the return.*

Virgil

The journey of the dead

Greek mythological tradition explained how two brothers acted over humanity in similar ways but with opposite results. *Hypnos* (Dream) and *Thanatos* (Death) fought over their victims, and when Thanatos won, the soul was transported to the Underworld, located in the extreme west and separated from the land of the living by the waters of the River Acheron, a branch of the River Styx. The Acheron flowed in Epirus, and becomes lost in a deep ravine during its course. Etymologically, it means 'the waters of pain', and it was considered the river of the Underworld due to its sinister appearance and its disappearance into the depths of the earth. To explain its origin, the Greeks invented a legend that tells how *Acheron*, the son of Helios and Gaea, offered water to the Titans that had rebelled against Zeus, and in vengeance, the god sent him into Tartarus. In Latin literary texts, we can find Acheron used to depict the depths of the Underworld.

The *River Cocytus* was a branch of the Acheron and also flowed into the Underworld. It was said that its flow increased with the tears of bad-hearted people who regretted their wicked deeds. On the shores of the Cocytus wandered the souls of the dead who had not received any burial ceremony and were awaiting the judges' decision about the punishment they were to receive.

To cross the river, the spirits of the deceased had to pay a fare to *Charon*, the ancient, squalid boatman. Before the descent into Tartarus, generous relatives would place a coin under the tongue of the deceased, and the spirits that had no coin were unable to pay their fare and were forced to remain on the near shore or to ask for assistance from Hermes, the Guide, and enter discreetly by the back gate.

Charon, according to legend, was the immortal son of Erebus and Night. He was mean and unbending in not allowing anybody without fare to board his ferry. Moreover he was cruel and merciless to those who had not been properly buried. Their rejected souls were condemned to wander for one hundred years, after which they were allowed to board the ferry free of charge.

On crossing the river in the rickety old boat, the dead arrived at the gates of the Underworld, guarded by *Cerberus*, the three-headed dog who sprouted a swarm of snakes instead of a tail, who let all enter, but none leave.

Once over the threshold to the Underworld, there was a great hall presided by the judges, *Minos*, *Aeacus*, and *Rhadamanthus*, who passed judgement over the new arrivals, assigning either the paradise of the Elysian Fields or the accursed Tartarus to each soul, according to its merits or faults. As they passed their verdicts, the spirits received the instructions to follow one of three paths: one which returned to the Asphodel Fields, in the first region of Tartarus where the souls of heroes wander aimlessly amongst the many other less-distinguished souls who flutter like bats, a place where those who are neither virtuous nor wicked remain. The second path led to the punishments of Tartarus, where the evil were sent, and the third path led the virtuous and good to the Elysian Fields.

The Elysium was governed by Cronus and located near the domain of Hades, though it did not form a part of it. It was a happy land, where it was neither hot nor cold, and the games and music never ceased. Nearby was the Island of the Fortunate, reserved for those who had been born and died three times and three times had been directed to the Elysium.

Analysis of the god Hades

As we have seen, it was not Hades who made decisions about where dead souls should go, or whether they were good or wicked, a decision made by the three judges. Hades simply ruled over this twilight world, though as its king, there were times when he had the last word in complicated decisions. Hades was feared, but just, the god of life and death – a double characteristic possessed by most of the mythological gods of the Inferno. He was also the duality of Good and Evil.

In Greek religion, death was rarely personified. Neither Hades nor Persephone was identified with death, despite being the gods of Tartarus and having ferocious and stern characters. In fact, in ancient times, death was an abstract term and represented the fear felt in the face of the unknown. The extremely minuscule cult that the Greeks worshipped, under the form of offerings, was a necessary homage offered to the souls that had been emancipated from the limits of the known world and had entered into direct communication with the gods. However, the cult was not the expression of a fearful religion of a specific god called Death.

PLUTO, THE GOD OF THE UNDERWORLD

In his primitive origins, Pluto, whose name is derived from the word 'ploutos', meaning 'wealth', was the personification of the fertility of the land, and the protector of abundant harvests. He was also known by his Latin name 'Dis Pater', or 'father of wealth'. He was soon assimilated with Hades, the Greek god of the Underworld, as he was also the proclaimed god of the dead and the riches that were found under the earth in the form of precious metals and stones. As the king of the Underworld, Pluto acquired a terrible character and inspired great fear in the Romans.

The people never attempted to contact him directly nor invoke him in case he appeared. In fact, they prayed fervently to never see his face. As a result of this, Pluto had no temples, and statues were rarely erected in his honour. When he was represented, he was given the form of a severe man with a sombre face, dark hair, and a beard, wearing a crown and bearing a sceptre and a key, which demonstrated the care with which he guarded those who entered his realm, and how vain was any hope of leaving.

Pluto was offered human sacrifices on occasion, but the sacrifices were generally of dark coloured animals, such as black sheep or pigs, in the festivals held in his honour called the Secular Games. These games were celebrated every hundred years, and all those condemned to death were consecrated to his terrible rage.

The journey to his kingdom, that all humans had to make sooner or later, was a difficult voyage of no return. According to tradition, the Romans only could make the journey across the *Avernus*. This lake, like the swamp of Lerna or Lake Amsanctus, was at the side of a headland close to Cumae and had been formed in the crater of an extinct volcano. The Romans believed that it communicated with the underground world where Pluto reigned, for its corrupt waters let off mephitic steam that killed any bird that flew through its path. The lake was surrounded by immense trees, whose branches were bent over the surface of the water to form a dome through which not a single ray of light penetrated. Close to the damned shores, the oracle of the shadows could be consulted.

Like the Greeks, the Romans left a coin under the tongue of their dead relatives so they could pay the ferryman. In Latin he also was called *Charon*, and he owned the only boat available. It was a leaking, worm-eaten old boat, which Charon ferried from one shore to the other. But the greedy ferryman would admit no soul who lacked the fare of a small coin called an *obolus*. It was said that there was always a large crowd of spirits and souls awaiting the journey across, as the current of the river was so strong that not even the strongest swimmer could have swum it. Charon, however, selected his passengers from those waiting. The Romans were inspired by the winged demon Hermes to create a more defined image of the Greek Charon, who was an uncertain character in their mythology.

Aside from Lake Avernus and River Acheron, there were other sacred waters in the Underworld, such as the *Phlegethon*, which according to the Romans separated Tartarus from the rest of the subterranean world. In this stretch of the current, the waves were of fire not of water. The *Lethe* was a blessed river, whose waters had the power to make anybody who drank them forget unpleasant thoughts, and thus prepared them for their happy stay in the Elysium.

The Romans also adopted the myth of Cerberus, the three-headed guardian dog, who ensured that no living being entered the Underworld and that no soul returned to the world of the living.

Like Hades, Pluto was accompanied by Proserpine in his throne room, from which all the infernal rivers flowed. It was there that the souls were judged by the three judges: Minos, Rhadamanthus, and Aeacus. The deeds of the souls were weighed in the Scales of Justice, and if the bad outweighed the good, the souls were sent on the burning current of the Phlegethon and taken by Nemesis, the goddess of revenge, to the flames of *Tartarus*.

Guilty souls were also handed over to the Furies, the three sisters who had the forms of serpents, and who drove them while stinging them with their tails. However, the good souls were taken to the *Elysian Fields*, far from the lamentable sights and terrible sounds of Tartarus. In the Elysian Fields, everything was beautiful and splendid, lit by its own sun and moon. There, it was always springtime and was adorned with the most fragrant and colourful blooms.

> *Hermes of plumed feet appeared sublime*
> *Beyond the tips of the tall trees*
> *In less time than it took*
> *To unload the slanting grain storm...*
> *Only the lawn lightly rustled its stems, and toward*
> *The sky, had flown swift before a sigh.*

> Keats

11. HERMES, THE WINGED GOD

Hermes was the son of Zeus and Maia, one of the seven Pleiades, daughters of Atlas. He was born in a cave on

Mount Cyllene, in Arcadia, and grew very fast. He showed, from when he was just a baby, a surprising quickness and extraordinary intelligence and cunning. It was said that he was only a few days old when he climbed out of his crib while his mother was looking away, and went to Pieria, where Apollo looked after an excellent herd of cattle, in search of adventure. He took the herd purely for his amusement, but he feared their hooves and, so, fashioned shoes from the bark of a fallen oak and tied to them to the cows' feet. Back at his cave, he found an empty turtle shell on the floor. He turned it over and tied strings across the resonant shell, making the first lyre.

Meanwhile, Apollo, who had discovered the disappearance of his cattle, but not that they had been taken deliberately, was looking for them. His search was unsuccessful, until, passing through Arcadia, he heard a beautiful melody. Following it, he found the baby Hermes and his herd. Apollo took Hermes to Olympus and reported him to Zeus for robbery, because two beasts were missing. Hermes explained that he had cut them up into twelve equal parts to make sacrifices to each of the gods (considering himself as the twelfth). This was the first animal sacrifice ever made. According to this story, Hermes was the youngest of the gods, at least younger than Apollo and Artemis. But other legends tell that he was born before them.

But, sticking with the first legend, Apollo forgave Hermes, and Hermes gave him the lyre in return for his herd. Later, Hermes took some rushes from the river and fashioned a flute. Apollo, enchanted once again by the instrument, offered to exchange it for a golden staff that he used to shepherd, which later became the famous *Caduceus*. In this way, Hermes became the god of all shepherds, but he also asked Apollo to teach him the art of foresight.

The young god, ingenious, eloquent, and persuasive, obtained all he desired. One day, he asked Zeus if he might be his herald and convinced him straight away. He was given a herald's wand that demanded everyone's respect, a round hat to protect him from the rain, and a pair of winged sandals which he used to travel from one place to another with the swiftness of the wind. Amongst his duties were

Hermes.

forming treaties, the promotion of trade, and the mainte-
nance of the right of free pass for travellers on all paths
world-wide.

His first task was to drive the dead to the realm of Hades
(he called the souls with delicateness and eloquence, placing
the golden staff over his eyes). Later, he became the god of
commerce and profit as the official herald of the gods, and
his participation in legends, as his influence over the gods,
humans, and the course of events, is by no means slight.

Hermes was an intelligent, cunning, if not sly, god. He
always said that he never lied, but that neither did he tell the
whole truth. He was, without a doubt, the most picturesque
of the Olympians. He learned the art of predicting the future
from the wet-nurse and masters of Apollo, observing the
movement of some pebbles in a jug of water. He invented
the game of jackstones and the art of using them to predict
the future. Hermes had several children, including *Echion*,
the herald of the Argonauts; *Autoclycus*, the thief; and
Daphnis, the inventor of bucolic poetry.

Analysis of the god Hermes

The Greeks viewed this eloquent, clever god as the
patron of prayers, the inventor of the alphabet, music,
astronomy, weights and measures (as he was the god of
trade), and gymnastics. Temples were often raised to him on
crossroads and on the roadside, as their presence alone
served to give courage to travellers and relief to wandering
tradesmen in their hard labour, as the god kept away the
dangers of travel and perilous encounters. Hermes was neither superhuman nor inhuman, but was the true divine
friend of the Greeks.

MERCURY, THE MESSENGER OF THE GODS

The primitive character of Mercury stands out clearly for
the significant etymology of his name: *merx*, from which

comes 'merchant', or '*mercari*', which means to traffic. This Roman god was therefore considered the god of trade and commerce. However, no legend has been found that links this attribute to him.

When the Roman gods were Hellenised, Mercury was identified with Hermes and adopted both his attributes and the legends that were told about him, such as the tale of the theft of Apollo's cattle. The Roman version tells how the young Mercury, who was hungry, discovered the herd in a wide meadow, but for the Romans Apollo was the god of the sun.

When Apollo discovered his fifty head of cattle were missing, he began looking for evidence that would lead him to identify the thief, but all he found were a few broken twigs. Then he remembered that a baby had been born in a cave a few days before, who had been named the king of thieves. Mercury was judged in Olympus and ordered to return the herd to Apollo, but as the hungry child had eaten two of the cattle, he gave Apollo the lyre that he had made on the day he was born.

Analysis of the legend

With this legend the Romans explain how Apollo (the Sun) possessed extensive herds of cattle and sheep (the clouds). Mercury personified the wind that, born during the night, becomes strong enough in the space of a few hours to blow the clouds away and hide them, returning them to the Sun the following morning.

* * *

According to Roman tradition, Apollo was so pleased with his lyre that he gave Mercury a magic wand called *Caduceus*, which had the power to reconcile any conflictive element. Anxious to try the wand, he placed it between two fighting serpents, which immediately curled around the wand in harmony. From then on the *Caduceus* was considered as the emblem of peace, concord, trade, and medicine.

When, due to his eloquence, Mercury was named the messenger of the gods, he was granted a pair of winged sandals, called *Talaria*, with which he flew with great speed. He was also given a winged hat, called *Petasus*, which gave him incredible rapidity of movement.

* * *

In the legend of Io, Mercury was sent by Jupiter to kill his guardian, the giant Argos, armed with no more than a fistful of poppies. Mercury approached Argos, and offered to tell him a story. The giant was happy to accept, for Mercury was considered the prince of eloquence, stories, and narrative. However, Mercury told him such long and tedious tales that the giant gradually fell asleep. Then Mercury spread the poppies about his head, sending Argos into a deep slumber, took up his great sword and, in one swipe, slit his throat.

Mercury was also in charge of driving the dead souls to the Underworld. For this task, he was called *Psicopompus*, while in his role as the carrier of dreams he was known as *Oneicopompus*. In this way, he became one of the most important gods of the Roman Parthenon. Not only was he the messenger of all the gods, but he also was credited as the god of eloquence, commerce, the wind and rain, and the special care of travellers, shepherds, cheaters, and thieves.

The Romans attributed him with the paternity of the *Lares* gods, the protectors of pathways, and of *Evandrus*, the founder of an Arcadian city situated at the foot of Mount Palatino. He was honoured with numerous temples, altars, and sanctuaries throughout the ancient world, and annual and solemn festivals were held in Rome every year called the Mercuralia, celebrated in May, his mother's month. The sculptures of his image are many and varied and were considered sacred, limiting signs; their extraction was punishable by death. Currently, his image appears in many public places, such as in Piccadilly Circus in London, or as a logotype for services from newspapers to telephone companies.

114

Apollo with your shining hair! You who are a
Blessing to the world, whose strong heart
Beats always with love, and light, and life.

Pike

12. APOLLO, THE BEAUTIFUL, TERRIBLE GOD

The birth of Apollo and Artemis

Leto, the daughter of the Titans Coeus and Phoebe, was
seduced by Zeus, and from their union were born the twins
Apollo and Artemis. Fearing the wrath of his wife, Zeus left
his lover, but Hera was not satisfied with that, and, in
vengeance, she ordered all the lands to refuse Leto any hospitality. Moreover, she asked the Earth to create a monster
that would pursue and mortify her. The monster was a serpent called *Phaethon*. Leto wandered around all the conti-
nents for months, unable to rest from her flight, and finally
arrived at an island called Ortygia that floated on the water.
The desolate, arid isle offered asylum to Leto, for she was
suffering the pains of labour. But neither Hera nor Eileithyia would help her in the birth, and Leto suffered with the
labour for nine days and nights, until Eileithyia took pity on
her and helped her to give birth to the twins. In the end, the
island became attached to the ocean bed with columns, and
its barren soil sprouted flowers and vegetation. From then
on it was called *Delos*, 'The Brilliant', and became one of
the most beautiful and fertile islands of the Cyclades.

* * *

Apollo was brought up by the goddess Themis, who fed
him on nectar. After a few days he asked for a bow and
arrows, and he went to Mount Parnassus, where he found
and shot the serpent Phaethon, who had pursued his mother.
Gravely wounded, Phaethon fled to seek shelter with the

115

oracle of Mother Earth in Delphi, but Apollo followed him to the sanctuary, where he finally killed him.

Mother Earth asked Zeus for justice, and Zeus not only ordered Apollo to go to the temple to purify himself, but also instigated the Pythian Games in honour of the serpent. Another version of the legend tells that Apollo himself founded the Games, in memory of his victory, and adopted the name Apollo Phaethon. The games were held every three years in Delphi.

Instead of going to the temple, Apollo preferred to go to Tarrha in Crete, where King Carmanor carried out the purification ceremony. When he returned to Greece, Apollo sought out Pan, the adoptive brother of Zeus, and, by using flattery, persuaded him to teach him the art of prophecy. He then overpowered the oracle of Delphi. From then on, Apollo, with knowledge of the truth and total sincerity, became the supreme carrier of the divine oracles. Perhaps this led to his later identification with the sun, which sees all from its place in the skies.

One day, when Leto was in a sacred forest, carrying out a private ceremony, *Tityus* the giant and son of Zeus appeared and tried to rape her. Apollo and Artemis, who heard her screams for help, ran to where she was and killed Tityus. Zeus, rather than being angry at his son's death, considered the act as one of pity. In Tartarus, Tityus was tortured as a punishment. His arms and legs were tied to the ground while two vultures devoured his liver.

Apollo was the symbol of masculine beauty and youth, but he was also a cruel god, wise and implacable to his enemies and even to his lovers. However, Apollo's most important function was his patronage of the arts, especially music. His myth tells how he was given the lyre by Hermes. Apollo showed such skill and harmony when he played the instrument, that the Muses became part of his entourage. Blessed with extraordinary sensitivity, Apollo could not bear unpleasant or imperfect melodies, but what he really could not tolerate was that anybody was better than him in any way.

Apollo.

The legend of Marsyas and the flute

One day, Athena made a flute from the bones of a crow and started to play it. The music produced by the flute was beautiful, but she was surprised when Hera and Aphrodite, who passed by, started to laugh when they saw her. Then she saw her image in a clear puddle while she was playing and realised that her face contorted into a ridiculous expression, her cheeks puffed up with air, when she played. Furious, she threw the flute from her and put a curse on it for whoever may pick it up. It was the satyr *Marsyas* who found the cursed flute, and as soon as it touched his lips, it was inspired by the music of Athena and started to play by itself. The satyr travelled through Phrygia, charming the ignorant country people, who exclaimed in delight that even Apollo could not play better. Apollo heard and became angry. He challenged Marsyas to a contest in which the winner would choose the loser's forfeit, and Marsyas, believing himself invincible, accepted the challenge.

When the contest ended in a draw, the cunning Apollo suggested they make it more difficult by playing and singing at the same time. This, of course, was impossible for Marsyas, and Apollo took his revenge by skinning him alive and hanging his skin on a pine tree near the source of the river that now bears his name.

* * *

One of Apollo's tasks, as part of a punishment set by Zeus, was to guard the herd and livestock of king Admetus. He also looked after the god's cattle, though this job was later delegated to Hermes. For a time, these tasks led to him being worshipped as the god of the protector of the flock.

Though Apollo refused to tie himself down in marriage, he had several love affairs, and various mortal women and nymphs bore his children. His first lover was *Coronis*, the daughter of Phlegyas, king of the Lapiths. Apollo fell in love with her one day when she was bathing in a lake in Thessaly. But in his absence, the girl fell in love with Ischys, the son of King Elatus of Arcadia. Apollo was mad with love and jealousy, and he shot his lover in the chest with his arrows. But when he saw her dead before him, he was sorry and bestowed funeral honours upon her body. He pulled his child, *Sculapius*, from her stomach just as Coronis began to be consumed by flames. He entrusted the child to Chiron, the wise centaur, who taught him the art of mixing medicines. In a short while, he became very skilled and was able to cure the sick and revive the dead. *Glaucus, Tyndareus*, and *Hippolyte* all owed him their return to life. But Hades complained that Sculapius was stealing his subjects, and Zeus struck him down with lightning as a punishment. Apollo, in revenge for the death of his son, killed the Cyclops, the makers of the lightning, and Zeus responded by exiling him to the Earth for a period, which was when he served King Admetus.

Amongst his other lovers are *Theia*, the muse *Thalia, Aria,* and *Cyrene*. But in spite of his beauty, Apollo did not always triumph in his attempted love affairs. On one occasion he tried to steal Idas' wife, *Marpessa*, but she remained faithful to her husband. He also pursued *Daphne*, the mountain nymph, daughter of king Peneus of Thessaly and a priestess of Mother Earth. When he tried to seduce her, she asked Mother Earth for help, who turned her into a laurel tree. With the leaves of the tree she made a crown for Apollo, with which he is often represented. From then on, the laurel was Apollo's favourite tree, and the prizes he awarded to poets, musicians, and other artists were crowns of laurel. Apollo also fell in love with a man, the Spartan prince Hyacinth, who was also loved by the poet Thamyris, the first man to court another man.

Analysis of the god Apollo

Apollo is the symbol of beauty, the perfection of form, and in some languages derived from Latin his name is used as an adjective to describe masculine beauty, like Adonis. He was considered the god of masculine beauty, music, poetry, and fine arts, as well as the protector of cattle and sheep. The Greeks multiplied his attributes, and on some

119

occasions, he was given a solemn character. He often was considered the god of instant punishment, as all sudden death is the result of his arrows. At times, he has condemned the human race to a slow and horrible death by sending a plague.

However, in the eyes of the other gods, Apollo was a friendly god and the main representative of prophecy and divination. Pity spoke in his name. It certainly could be said that, for the Greeks, Apollo reflected the artistic spirit of their land and the ideals of youth, beauty, and progress.

APOLLO, THE SUN GOD

Apollo was the only Greek god who conserved his original name when he was adopted by the Romans. There are scarcely any variations between the Roman and Greek Apollo, except that, for the Romans, he was not only the god of medicine, music, poetry, and fine arts, the symbol of masculine beauty and youth, but also the god of the sun, by which he also adopted the attributes and legends of the Greek Sun god *Helios*. The Romans justified this with the explanation that Apollo was the son of Jupiter, the sky, and Leto, the night, and had been born in Delos, which means bright earth.

Apollo was given three other names: *Phoebe*, 'the lord of light and life', *Cynthius,* and *Pythius*. Like all the other sun gods, he was represented as an athletic young man, with shining blond hair, and armed with fearful weapons that he used for both good and bad deeds, depending on his mood, just as the sun can be both beneficial and harmful.

The Ancient Romans' version of the legend of *Phaethon* is different from the one told in Greece. It tells that Apollo wanted to free the human race from its evils, and the monstrous serpent Phaethon was one of these, born from the dirty and stagnant waters that remained under the Earths surface after the great fold. His victory over the serpent, which nobody had dared to challenge until then, earned him the name Pythius meaning 'Killer'.

13. ARTEMIS, THE GODDESS OF THE HUNT

Artemis was characterised with the same features and attributes as her brother. Like him, she was armed with a bow and arrow, which she used without pity to kill anyone who, in one way or another, dared to insult herself or her mother. She also had the power to send plague or sudden death to mortals and to heal them. She was considered the protector of small children and of all suckling animals, but she was principally the virgin goddess of the hunt. She ran through the forests with her bow always raised, accompanied by an entourage of fresh water nymph-spirits.

Unlike her brother, however, she decided to remain a virgin. Her modesty reached such levels that, one day, when she was bathing in a stream, a Theban youth called *Acteon*, who had become, under the instruction of Chiron, one of the greatest hunters of the land, passed that way and surprised her. Angry at his insolence, she first converted him into a crow and then incited her fifty hounds to devour him. According to some mythologists, the hounds represent the fifty days of the year when the vegetation, symbolised by Acteon, dies.

Artemis demanded the same chastity from her companions. On one occasion, she found out that *Callisto*, one of her nymphs, was pregnant by her father Zeus. She turned the nymph into a bear and called her hounds. The pack would have killed the bear had Zeus not trapped it and sent it into the skies, where he converted it into a constellation. Arcas, the child that was born, was able to save himself and became the king of the Arcadians.

Artemis was beautiful, chaste, temperamental, proud, and cruel – her father's daughter. She was named by the Moirae as the patron of births, as her mother Leto had given birth to her with no pain. As the goddess of the hunt, she lived in the forest, for which reason she was also considered the goddess of nature in its pure, wild state.

The temple of Artemis in Ephesus was considered one of the seven wonders of the Ancient world, with its incredible magnificence and enormous dimensions. On the same coast

The main temples honouring the beautiful god are found in Delos, where a priestess called Pythia proclaimed his infallible orations. Apollo also inspired many beautiful statues. He is generally represented as a young man, crowned with laurel leaves and holding a lyre. His most beautiful statue is said to be the 'Apollo Belvedere', where he is shown in the act of defeating Phaethon.

Analysis of the legends of Apollo

The explanation of the majority of the legends about Apollo is found in the symbolism offered by the Sun. In this way, Apollo's love for Coronis signifies the affinity of the Sun with the dawn, which, though loved by the Sun, falls under its brilliant, piercing arrows. As the Sun was naturally recognised as the restorer of life after the long destructive influence of winter and sickness, it is natural that the sunset, Sculapius, was given wonderful healing powers.

For the same reason, the Sun was supposed to be in constant struggle against cold and illness. The defeat of Phaethon was therefore an allegory that illustrates the healing and regenerative powers of the Sun, in drying out swamps and stagnant water, which prevented the spread of malaria.

In the legend of Daphne, whose name comes from 'Dahana', meaning 'dawn' in Sanskrit, we find a second version of the legend of Coronis, in which the Sun kills the dawn, even though he is in love with her. Mythologists interpret this legend as Daphne, the personification of the morning dew, being dissolved by the heat of the Sun's rays, leaving no trace but the green fields.

Near the Deium olive tree
Leto gave you life,
So that you would always be queen
Of the mountains and the green forests,
Of the mystery of each deep valley
And of all the currents and their melodies.

Catullus

Artemis.

of Asia Minor, the sanctuary of the goddess of the hunt was four times larger than that of Athena in Parthenon, and it is the place where, according to Jacob Burokhardt, East and West mysteriously and beautifully become one.

Analysis of the goddess Artemis

In ancient times, several Artemis were known. In Tauride, they worshipped a cruel goddess who rode in a chariot drawn by two bulls, carrying a torch and bearing a crescent moon on her forehead. Foreigners were sacrificed to her in a vicious custom from which it is said that *Orestes* was able to escape. The Artemis of Ephesus differed from the traditional goddess, for instead of denying love, she offered herself to it with no ties and fed humans and the Earth from her many breasts, filled with milk. However, despite these diversions, the Greek Artemis was chaste and a huntress, and she has these attributes in the vast majority of legends.

DIANA, THE GODDESS OF THE MOON

The Roman goddess was rapidly assimilated with the Greek Artemis, who according to some authors was introduced to Rome by the legendary king Servius Tulius. For this reason, most of the legends of the Roman goddess come from Greek mythology.

It is told that Orestes, the son of Agamemnon, carried the Artemis of Tauride to the city of Nemi in Italy. Indeed, there was a temple dedicated to the goddess Diana, next to a lake and a sacred forest. It is known that the temple was used for human sacrifices, and each priest, moreover, had to kill his predecessor in order to carry on the work. It is also said that Hippolyte, the son of Theseus who was brought back to life by Sculapius, was kidnapped by Artemis and taken to Italy, where he adopted the name *Virbius* in order to devote himself entirely to the cult of his divine kidnapper.

Diana.

Though the Roman goddess is represented as a beautiful young woman, dressed in hunting clothes and armed with a bow and a full quiver of arrows, she is also considered the sister god of Apollo, that is the moon. For this reason, she bears a half-moon on her forehead. The Romans believed that, as soon as the sun set and night fell, the beautiful goddess climbed aboard her lunar chariot and drove her white steeds across the skies, greeting the brilliant stars as she passed, which she cared for and loved. Sometimes she stopped to contemplate the Earth, for if nature seemed beautiful to her during the day, by night she thought it far more enchanting and adored its heady perfume.

> *In chorus we sing to the wine, sweet wine,*
> *To its soft strength and its rich flavour.*

Martínez de la Rosa

14. DIONYSUS, THE GOD OF WINE AND THEATRE

The birth of Dionysus

Zeus had an affair with the beautiful nymph *Semele*, the daughter of Cadmus and Harmonia. In order not to scare her away, Zeus took on the image of a mortal. Semele became pregnant, and when Hera found out about her husband's infidelity, she wanted to punish her. In the sixth month of her pregnancy, Hera disguised herself as an elderly neighbour and advised her to ask her lover not to deceive her any more and to reveal himself before her in his true form, because how was she to know that he was not a monster? Semele remembered that Zeus had promised her anything she wanted, and she followed the advice, curious to know the aspect of her lover. Zeus was terrified at her request, but could not refuse her, and so he showed himself to her with his thunder and lightning, and the woman was immediately struck down. But Zeus had time to take her child from her stomach, and Hermes put it in Zeus' thigh. Three months later, *Dionysus* was born from his father's leg. For this reason, Dionysus was known as *Demeter*, meaning 'he of two mothers', or 'twice-born', and also *Dithy Rambo*, 'the child of the double door'.

Though Semele was dead, Hera was not satisfied and threw all her hatred at Dionysus, the son of the mortal woman whom Zeus had loved more than any other. Zeus, to take Dionysus out of Hera's range, disguised him as a girl and handed him over to King Athamantis of Orchomenus and his wife Ino. But Hera was not fooled, and she punished the royal couple by driving them mad. Zeus then turned the child into a kid goat, and gave him to the nymphs Macris, Nysa, Erato, Bromie, and Bracche on Mount Nysa. Later Zeus put their images among the stars, creating the constellation called the *Hyades*.

When Dionysus reached adult age, Hera recognised him and drove him mad, so that he was destined to wander the earth, spreading the cult of the vine and the way to obtain wine, which he had invented as a child on Mount Nysa and for which he is most famous. Dionysus wandered around with his tutor *Silenus* and an unorganised army of satyrs, armed with an ivy covered wand with pine needles on the end, called the *"thyrsus"*, and with serpents, posts, and swords. They drank wine and, inebriated, danced madly.

Dionysus sailed to Egypt, where he had his first military victory with the help of the Amazons, over the Titans, and restored the kingdom of King Ammon. Then he set sail for India, which he conquered and showed its people the art of harvesting vines, imposed law, and founded great cities. Then he returned to Europe, where his grandmother Rhea purified him, passing him through Phrygia. He later invaded Thrace, where he found himself opposed by Lycurgus. But his grandmother wanted to help him and drove Lycurgus mad, who in delirium murdered his own son, and the entire land became barren. When Dionysus announced that the barrenness would continue whilst the king was alone, the Edonians decided to kill the king. Dionysus met no further opposition in Thrace, and he continued his voyage to

127

Thebes, where he tried to establish his cult. But King Pentheus stood against him, and his mother, Agave, cut him up in a fit of madness.

When all Boeotia had recognised Dionysus' triumph, the god turned to the Aegean islands, offering joy and terror wherever he set foot. Then he took a ship to Naxos, but his crew, made of pirates, tried to mutiny, with the idea of selling him as a slave at the next port. As soon as Dionysus realised their intentions, he filled the ship with ivy so that it could no longer sail and blew his flute with resonant blasts. Terrified, the pirates jumped overboard and became dolphins.

In Naxos, Dionysus met the lovely *Ariadne*, who had been abandoned by Theseus, and he married her straight away. They had several children: *Oenopion, Thaos, Staphylos, Latrimis, Errante,* and *Tauropolus*. From then on, the divine activities of Dionysus were centred on introducing orgiastic cults to all the regions in her honour, which were closely related to religious rites, and of which traces are still found within the celebrations of the grape harvest in some places. The rites were called the *Bacchanalias* and were collective festivities that mixed dancing and historical acting representations with popular entertainment and games. These dramatic representations led him to be considered the god of theatre and comedy.

Finally, his cult was implanted in Greece, and before going to Olympus, he descended into the Underworld and rescued his mother, deceiving Hades, and took her with him to Olympus, where they both were converted in immortals, and she was given the name *Thyone*.

The Apollonian versus the Dionysian

Friedrich Nietzsche, the German philosopher (1844-1900), identified two attitudes toward life for which he took terms from Greek mythology. He also used the terms to represent his own conceptions of aesthetics: the Apollonian and the Dionysian. The Apollonian is light, balanced, individual, restrained, and limited, while the Dionysian is instinc-

Dionysus and Silenus.

tive and irrational, the collective current of life, and the affirmation of the will to live unrestrictedly. This ideal is appropriately represented by theatre and music.

Dionysus' entourage

Dionysus was the only god who was never found alone, as his *Thyasos*, or entourage, were always at his side. The group was made up of various assistants: *Silenus*, his tutor, who was known as wise, philosophical, and a prophet, as the wine gave him the power of seeing into both the past and the future. He was an old man, ugly and podgy, and was usually drunk and mounted on an ass.

The *satyrs* had tangled hair, pointed ears, two horns on their foreheads, and sometimes a horse's tail. Their legs, and at times the tail, were like those of a Billy goat. They were also called fauns, and they ran incessantly through the countryside looking for sexual adventure, for which they were feared by humans.

Menade in Greek means manic or crazy, and in plural it means furious. When the mysteries of Dionysus were celebrated, the Bacchantes or Menades were taken over by an uncontrollable madness. They stripped naked or semi-naked, crowned in ivy, and danced frenetically until they became delirious.

Analysis of the god Dionysus

The cult of Dionysus is related to wine and drunkenness and, together with the cult of the vine, extended all over Greece. The god became the personification of the inebriating power of nature and of the life force that flows though the grape vines and gives life to all plants. In the classic period, he also was worshipped as the god of joyful life, parties, delirium, and orgies. It is also significant that the Greeks considered him the protector god of fine arts and, in particular, tragic and comic drama, which were always represented in the celebrations of his cult.

130

The myth of Dionysus is also related to madness, as from his birth, many of the people around him were driven mad by the gods. In his festival, the Bacchanals, his followers even reached an ecstasy that granted them super and terrible strength, at the hands of which some heroes suffered, for in a full frenzy they could rip apart and devour animals or people.

Dionysus was called Bacchus by the Romans, as well as *Bromius*, which meant bellow or roar, as he was able to turn himself into a lion or a bull. In his honour, ritual chants such as the 'evohe' and the 'dithyramb' were sung.

Dionysus was not born a god, as his mother was mortal, but he became one, in the process called apotheosis. Semele changed her name at the same time as her status, supposedly to avoid the wrath of Hera. There is also an explanation for this in ancient cultures, which considers that a person's name is very important for knowing and identifying them.

Dionysus was a friendly, joyful god, though some of his acts of vengeance were cruel and terrible. He was called the sweetest and the cruellest of humans.

The symbolism of his voyages is that like him, vines and wine were not originally from Greece. This myth therefore explains how they arrived from other places, as the principal crop of Greece was the olive and its oil, with which Athena obtained her spiritual possession of the land.

The myth of Orphism

Orphism was a religious sect born in Ancient Greece in the sixth century BC. Its creation was attributed to the mythical poet Orpheus. The sect practised rituals of which the organisation and evolution have never been fully discovered. The success of orphism in Greece is rooted in its tendency to extract the complexity that made mythology almost incomprehensible and to harmonise different gods, myths, and religious doctrines to better emphasise the idea of a single god, who in that period was called *Zeus*, or more often *Zagreus*.

According to orphic tradition, the soul is immortal, but inhabits a mortal body, and therefore introduced three new elements: passion, death, and resurrection. This is explained by the myth of Dionysus Zagreus, son of the god Zeus and the mortal Semele. As a child, Dionysus was kidnapped by the Titans on Hera's orders, cut up into tiny pieces, and made into stew, from which sprouted a pomegranate tree. The fruits of the tree opened as though they were wounds, and from them came red seeds. The pomegranate is the symbol of resurrection, and it usually appears as such in sepulchral iconography.

BACCHUS, THE GOD OF WINE AND FUN

Bacchus was the Roman god of wine and the vine and of fun, frenzy, and freedom. Much like Dionysus, he had no important role in Roman religion. However, he was worshipped and adored across the land, and innumerable festivals were held in his name. In Italy, the most famous were the Dionysus Major and Minor and the Liberalia, which gave free reign to unrestrained and frenetic celebrations. But in Rome, he was worshipped by fewer people, who abandoned themselves to orgies in the bacchanal rituals, which the senate unsuccessfully tried to ban.

The most devoted of Bacchus' followers were women called the *Bacchantes*, who maintained a perpetual state of celebration and inebriation. Though they were not priestesses, they had an important role in Roman religion and in the cult, and were mostly seen at the bacchanals and the festivals held in the god's honour.

15. JANUS, THE GOD WITH TWO FACES

Janus, who was completely unknown by the Greeks, was one of the most important members of the Roman pantheon, and even had a certain pre-eminence over Jupiter. He was the Roman god of the past, the present, and the future; of doorways, entrances, and bridges; and patron of all origins.

There are several versions of the story of his origins and

132

birth. Some legends tell that he was the son of Apollo. Though he was born in Thessaly, he soon left for Italy, where he founded a city on the Tiber, which he named *Janiculus*. There, he was united with Saturn, the Greek counterpart of Cronus, who had been exiled by Jupiter and with whom he generously shared his throne. Together they civilised the savage inhabitants of Italy, blessing them with such prosperity that their kingdom was known as the Golden Age.

Other mythologists tell that the god arrived in Italy as the captain of a fleet of ships, and settled in Lazio, where he founded Janiculum, after his own name. He made Saturn welcome in his kingdom, who, in thanks, granted him the gift of the 'double science' of the past and the future.

This is why Janus is represented with two faces that look in opposite directions. Some statues show one face with white hair and beard and the other with a young appearance, while other images give him three or even four heads and represent him as the god of the four seasons.

He is considered the emblem of the sun, which opens the day with its rising and closes it with its setting. For this reason he was the guardian god of doorways, as every door looks two ways (Janus Bifrons). In war time, the doors of his sanctuary were left permanently open, so that the god could attend the Romans' needs at any time. The doors were only closed once the war was over, and in peace time, to show that the intervention of the god was no longer necessary and that he had returned to his sanctuary. The Romans, however, were such a belligerent people that, throughout more than seven centuries, the doors were left closed only three times and only for brief periods each time.

The god's attributions gradually increased, and he became the god of all origins: the beginning of each new year, month, and day were considered sacred to him, and he was offered prayers and sacrifices at these sacred times. In religious ceremonies, his name was the first pronounced, as he was the only one who presided over the doors through which the human prayers to the gods could arrive. For this reason, he often was represented with a key, sometimes in his right hand, sometimes in his left, and when he presided over the years, he held the number three hundred in one hand and sixty-five in the other.

One of the most famous temples dedicated to the glory of Janus was a totally square building known as the *Janus Cuadrifons*. On each side of the building there was a door and three windows, which symbolised the four seasons and the twelve months when opened. The festivals held in Janus' honour were celebrated on the first day of each nine year period. As the god of origin he was consecrated the first month of the year, *Januarius*, which was a sacred month for the Romans, when they had the custom of exchanging greetings, good wishes, and presents on the first day of the month. This custom is still practised by the Italian people.

Ovid said that Janus had a double life, as he executed his double power over both the earth and the sky. He was not considered a cosmogonic god, simply a Roman god, and the symbol of the vigilance over the powerful city, where goods were carried by the Tiber in both directions. The diversity of his attributions show to what point he was the essential god of the world that opened and shut, at his will, and where nothing escaped his attention.

IV

MINOR GODS AND
COLLECTIVE DIVINITIES

Apart from the Olympian gods, there were other, less important gods, who nevertheless played a vital role in Greek mythology. There also existed other forces that usually manifested themselves as a collective. They each deserve a brief description, and we will see here the most significant.

> *He is great and just,*
> *He is always good, and therefore*
> *Should be honoured, narcissi*
> *Roses, cloves and lilies*
> *Always honoured! Always young.*
> *The great Pan is always praised!*

> Beaumont and Fletcher

1. PAN THE RURAL FLAUTIST, AND OTHER DEITIES OF NATURE

There are several versions of the origins of Pan. One tells that he was the son of Cronus and Rhea, which makes him one of the most ancient gods; another says he was the son of

Zeus and Hybris; and yet another that his parents were Hermes and Penelope. However, the two most respected legends tell that Pan was either the adoptive son of Zeus and was raised in the cave of Dicte on Mount Aegeus, where he was suckled by the goat Amalthea; or that he was the son of Hermes and a nymph from Arcadia, Dryope or Oenis. It is told that his appearance was so strange that his mother abandoned him at birth and ran away, and when his father presented him to the other gods and they saw a bearded kid with hooves and horns, they burst into laughter. But Pan not only made people laugh, he also had such a furious temper that he could terrify anybody with his savage strength.

Pan really was the least agreeable god, with his monstrous deformed appearance, half man and half animal, with the head and legs of a goat, a woolly body, a pointed goat's beard, and horns on his head. His physical appearance was later inherited by the Christian demon that tempted the saintly anchorites with lubricious visions and ardent fantasies.

Pan was the god of fecundity and sexual potency, both brutal in his desires and terrifying in his apparitions. His name is the root of the word panic. He was especially worshipped in Arcadia, but his cult soon spread over all of Greece, particularly during the classic period. At first, he was the protector of cattle, goats, and shepherds, and he generally helped hunters catch their prey. He was usually carefree and lazy; what he most enjoyed was napping, and he punished those who disturbed him with a sudden, terrifying scream that made their hair stand on end.

In spite of his unpleasant appearance and his spine-chilling scream, the people of Arcadia considered Pan to be a rural god of the mountains and fields, who shepherded goats and relaxed in the fields. He was not an evil god, but a rustic, cheerful god, though mischievous and wanton, and he often amused himself by chasing the wood nymphs. Some escaped his pursuit by metamorphosis. *Syrinx* turned herself into a cane, and the mischievous god made a set of pipes from her reeds, which he called 'syrinx' in her memory, to keep her close to his lips. *Pythia* transformed herself into a pine tree, and from it Pan took his green crown. Pan's best

Pan, Aphrodite and Eros.

conquest was *Selene*, who he seduced by hiding his goat like appearance under clean white robes.

Little by little, he acquired new attributes and became associated with several legends. Pan was also consecrated as a doctor, a healer, a prophet, and the inventor of the syringe and the Pan pipes. The Olympian gods, though they laughed at his terrible appearance, made the most of his powers. Apollo took from him the art of seeing the future, and Hermes copied the design of his flute, declaring that it was his own invention.

The story of Syrinx

Pan had the same weakness for music as he did for pretty nymphs. On one occasion he fell in love with the nymph *Syrinx*, but she was frightened by his horrible appearance and fled. Pan was not put off and followed in pursuit. He was about to catch her when she sent Gaea a plea for assistance. As soon as the words left her mouth, she was transformed into a bush of reeds that the panting god grasped hold of before he realised the nymph had escaped.

He was so disappointed that he let out a long and deep sigh, which produced a melody of sad notes as it passed through the reeds. To preserve forever the memory of his nearly beloved, he broke off seven reeds of different lengths and tied them together, creating a musical instrument which he called by the beautiful nymph's name and have become known as Pan pipes. Afterwards, he left the pipes in a cave, where later, ladies would shut themselves in, and if they were virgins, would come out accompanied by the sweet melodies of the pipes, but if the were not, despite their insistence, they would disappear forever.

* * *

According to Roman legend, Pan had the name of *Consentes*, among others, and was considered the god of shepherds and the personification of nature. He would amuse himself by terrifying praying travellers with his piercing scream.

Analysis of the god Pan

Pan is one of the great unknown elements of Greek mythology. He was a doctor, a healer, a prophet, the inventor of the syringe and the pipes, and due to both his beastly appearance and his never-sated love, he was the manifestation of invincible force and nature. But his importance was concealed behind the more attractive gods.

Under the influence of neo-Platonic philosophy, Pan was associated with the idea of fertility, and it was supposed that he favoured the fertility of the livestock. The concept of total god (Pan means 'all') inspired Plutarch in the following tale: in the reign of Tiberius, an Egyptian sailor called Thamus who was sailing from Italy to Greece, heard one afternoon opposite the coast of Epirus a strange voice that said to him, "the great Pan is dead". The voice repeated this three times, adding the mysterious order, "When you reach the coast of Palodes announce the death of the great Pan". After much consideration, Thamus obeyed the voice. From the prow of the boat, facing the land, he stood and shouted, "The great Pan is dead!" Then, Plutarch tells, hardly had the words left his mouth, when a great sob arose from many voices, mixed with shouts of surprise. Pan is the only god to have died, and according to Christian authors, his death signifies the death of Paganism, which was then substituted by Christianity.

Apart from Pan, the Romans worshipped other divinities that were completely unknown to the Greeks. Some examples are:

- *Sylvanus*. He was the Roman god of woods, orchards, and copses. First worshipped in the form of a tree, he was later given human form and became assimilated with the gods Pan and Faun. He had a malicious character and loved playing jokes on unsuspecting travellers who passed through the woods. Parents even used to threaten their children with the temper of the god to persuade them to behave. Though he was highly popular among rural peoples as a protective and pastoral god, he had no official cult. In general, he was represented with the features of a cheerful old man, crowned with ivy and holding a pair of secateurs. He was offered fruits and small animals.

- *Faun*. He is one of the oldest gods of Roman mythology. He was supposed to be the son of *Picus*, son of Saturn. He was attributed a double function: he frequented woods, cultivated plains, fresh water, and protected the crops and livestock, as well as pronounced oracles through the murmuring of the leaves, like his father, who possessed the gift of predicting the rain. He was represented with a beard and dressed in goat skins, carrying either a shepherd's crook or the horn of abundance, as he favoured the fertility of the fields. It was precisely for this reason that he was identified with Pan, after the systematic Hellenisation of the Roman gods and adopted the same characteristics as his Greek counterpart: the horns on his forehead and the goat hooves.

The fauns were the Roman equivalent of the Greek satyrs, which were descended from the god Faun, the grandson of Saturn. However, they were only demi-gods, and although they lived long lives, they were not immortal. Like Faun, they were represented with small horns, a tail, and goat hooves for feet.

- *Fauna*. She was the wife of the god Faun and protected women from sterility. She was also believed to be the mother of Latino, one of the legendary kings of Lazio.

- *Flora*. She was the goddess of flowers and the spring, worshipped by the Sabines. She was the most beautiful of the minor goddesses and was married to *Zephyr*, the amiable god of the south wind, at whose side she wandered from one place to another, dispersing the pleasant fragrance of flowers. It was believed that her husband had granted her powers over the blooms of spring. She was particularly worshipped by young people, who offered her fruits and garlands of flowers. Her festivals, called the Floralia, were usually held in May. Legend explains the reason for this celebration with the story that Flora offered Juno a beautiful flower that had the power of fertilising any woman who touched it. Juno became pregnant, and in her honour the Romans gave the child that was born with the name Mars, the first month of the spring.

- *Pryapus*. Called the god of the shadow, he was also considered a rural god, but was only known and worshipped along the banks of the River Hellespont.

Other rural gods were *Vertumnus* and *Pomona*, who were special divinities of gardens and fertile land. They were represented with pruning knives, garden sheers, and other gardening tools, fruits and flowers. They shared their divine labours, and one of their tasks was to turn the fruit over so that it was well exposed to the autumn sun.

- *Vertumnus*. He was a god who originated from Etruria and symbolised the changes that took place in nature, especially the change from blossom to fruit. His name comes from the Latin '*vertere*', which means 'to change'. The Romans took advantage of the etymology to create a legend in which Vertumnus fell in love with the beautiful nymph Pomona. To seduce her, the god took on several forms that represented the various seasons of the year: first he turned himself into a farmer, then a harvester, then a vine grower, and then he to took the form of a handsome man in the bloom of youth. All this succeeded in winning him the affections of the nymph, and they established a cult together, in which they received offerings of the first fruits and flowers of the year.

- *Pomona*. She was the Etruscan nymph of flowers and fruit and became incorporated into Roman religion. She was praised by many poets, who told of her many romantic affairs with rustic and agricultural gods, such as Pico and Sylvan. But Pomona was faithful to her husband Vertumnus. According to Ovid, the immortal fidelity that the two professed permitted them to recurrently grow old and recuperate their youth, just like the cycle of the seasons and the stages of the plants. Pomona was usually represented by artists seated on a great basket of fruits and flowers, sometimes wearing a crown of vines and twigs, while she served the fruit in a horn of abundance.

- *Pales*. A Latin pastoral divinity, sometimes a god and sometimes a goddess, he or she was the god of the meadows, flocks, and shepherds, who were then called the 'pupils' or 'favourites' of Pales by poets. On 21st April, the day that tradition says Rome was founded, the anniversary of the city was celebrated with festivals in honour of Pales, with the purpose of purifying the livestock and stables.

2. CYBELE, THE GODDESS OF FERTILITY

All the ancient civilisations worshipped a goddess who represented fertility. As fertility guaranteed the future of humanity, the goddesses of the Earth, or Mother Earth, took on a fundamental role in mythology. In Greek mythology, as we have seen, this role was first fulfilled by Gaea. However, the few attributions that she was given and her unspecified personality did not bring her much popularity, and views about her were confused, leading to her substitution by another divinity.

Cybele, the Great Mother of the peoples of Asia Minor, came to occupy the place left by Rhea. A cult that was orgiastic and bloody in its origins, with penitentiary and mortifying rites that sometimes went as far as ritual self-mutilation was dedicated to this Phrygian goddess. The origins of this cult came from an ancient legend of which several versions exist. Here we can examine that which is richest in detail; Zeus, the god of the skies, saw Cybele, the goddess of the Earth, and fell in love with her. But she was to be his, and so he put his semen on a stone, from which a hermaphrodite called *Agdistis* was born. But the gods decided to convert Agdistis into a woman and castrated her, burying the discarded genitals, from which sprouted an almond tree. One day, a daughter of the River Sangrarius ate an almond from the tree and fell pregnant, giving birth to a boy. She abandoned the child at birth, and he was brought up by a male goat. The child was named *Attis* and grew into a desirable youth, whose extraordinary beauty attracted both Cybele and even Agdistis herself. But Attis was destined to marry the daughter of the king, and so, Cybele drove him mad. In a frenzy, Attis castrated himself and died. Cybele regretted her actions, and asked Zeus that the body may remain uncorrupted and that the little finger remain alive. Then Cybele established an annual ritual in Attis' honour, whose priests had to be castrated in his memory.

The Phrygian goddess was, without a doubt, the major divinity of the Middle East. She was represented with all the splendour of a queen, and her chariot was drawn by two

Cybele.

lions, symbols of her strength, and which were, in reality, Atlanta and her lover Hippomaenes, who were punished for copulating in a temple of the goddess. Cybele carried a key that opened the gates of the earth where all her riches were buried, and on her head she wore a headdress with small towers, which represented the cities that she protected.

Analysis of the goddess Cybele

Cybele was given other names, such as Mother Earth, Earth, and Great Goddess, and she was the power of all wild plants and animals of the Earth. The legend of Cybele and Attis is very important to mythology, as it represents the origin or transposition of the orgiastic and orphic mysteries of the resurrection. In one version, Attis, who had sworn to his beloved Cybele that he would remain chaste, broke his promise, and she condemned him to madness in revenge. He cut off his genitals at the foot of a pine tree, where violets sprang from the spilled blood. Another version tells that the pine tree itself sprang from the blood. This is significant symbolism, because it relates the pine and the pine cone to funerary images.

When she saw that Attis had died, Cybele wrapped him in strips of linen like a mummy, and revived him. From then on she became the goddess of life and death, and she developed an important cult, repeating the orphic theory that we saw with Dionysus.

The *Galli*, the priests of Cybele, were castrated in honour of Attis. Once initiated, they would re-enact the myth of Attis in the festivals named after him, in which a pine tree was felled, sold, and carried in procession to the temple on Palatine Hill. The branches that remained outside were decorated with violets. On the 22nd March, the equinox, the tree was placed on a bench, and the festivities were held during the morning.

* * *

The people of the ancient world feared hunger, and the

rains were considered vital for a good harvest. Agriculture was much more important to the Romans than commerce, for abundant harvests signified the survival of civilisation. For this reason, the gods of plants and fertility were multiplied. For example, they worshipped Ceres as the goddess of the harvest; Pryapus as the god of orchards and copses; *Ops* and *Copia* as divinities of abundance; Flora, who favoured the fertility of flowers; and Pomona and Vertumnus, who ripened the fruit.

Ops was Saturn's wife and the goddess of abundance. She was identified with Cybele and Rhea and figured among the numerous Roman divinities of the Earth. According to one legend, Ops was introduced in the Roman pantheon by Titus Tatius, the head of the Sabines. It was supposed that she protected the crops, and her public festival was held at the time of sowing and when the harvest was gathered. She was later represented with the features of a seated matron who offered her right hand in aid and gave bread with her left.

She was also worshipped as the goddess *Bona Dea*, the principal divinity of fertility. She was invoked and worshipped strictly by Roman women, who gave thanks to the goddess for their numerous children or asked the goddess to make them fertile, and she allowed them to be mothers.

The emperors venerated the allegorical goddess *Fecundity*, to whom they prayed for a strong line of descendants, with the first child being a son, so as to ensure the perpetuity of the Roman State. Domestic animals were also placed under the protection of the goddess of fertility or other gods, such as Faun or Pales, who ensured that they bred rapidly and often. The Roman people solicited protection and aid from all their fertility gods, by dedicating numerous statues and images to them, which they put in their gardens and fields, and by holding festivals in their honour on specific dates.

Hebe, honoured by all
Administered her nectar and with golden goblets
They toasted each other one and all.

Homer

3. HEBE, THE NECTAR SERVER OF OLYMPUS

Hebe was the daughter of Zeus and Hera, and the sister of Ares and Hephaestus, much more widely known than she, for her mythology is limited to her marriage to the hero Hercules. Hebe means youth, and it was supposed that her divine power lay in her ability to grant the gifts of eternal youth and immortality. She did this by serving nectar, the drink of the gods, for which reason she was known as the server of the gods.

She was also charged with the domestic chores of Olympus, and the legends referring to her are practically non-existent. One legend tells that one day she was pouring nectar, and she slipped and spilled it all. Zeus was furious, so he converted himself into an eagle, descended to Earth, and kidnapped Ganymede, the son of the king Tros, as a substitute for Hebe. A second version of this tale tells that when Hercules ascended to Olympus as an immortal, Hera conceded him the hand of Hebe as a conciliatory gesture. The couple had two sons, *Alexiares* and *Anicetus*.

* * *

Hebe was called *Juventas* by the Romans. She was the allegorical goddess of youth and was worshipped by youths when they first wore their togas as adults. She was also considered the patron of the difficult passage into the world of adulthood.

4. EILEITHYIA, THE MATRON GODDESS

Eileithyia was the least-known daughter of Zeus and Hera, charged with the task of presiding over all births. She was very close to her mother and was considered the goddess of maternity. She was supposed to have aided in labour, so that no woman could give birth without her being present.

In *The Iliad*, several Eileithyias are named, who personified different stages in childbirth. Eileithyia was represented as a young woman with one hand raised and the other holding a lit torch, the symbol of new life. Her most important role in mythology was in the birth of Leto, in which Hera had refused to help. In the end, Eileithyia took pity on Leto and gave her aid in the birth.

5. THE GODS OF DEATH

Nyx, the goddess of the night, bore on her own *Thanatos* (Death) and *Hypnos* (Dream). Her daughters were the *Moirae*, *Nemesis* (Revenge), and *Eris* (Discord). The brothers Thanatos and Hypnos acted in a similar way, though the effects were completely opposite. When Thanatos won over his brother, the victim was transported to the reign of Hades.

Both brothers were represented as handsome youths, who carried the mysterious symbols of the dish and the torch. Hypnos, as the personification of sleep, was a gentler version of Thanatos, personification of death. Hesiod said that the winged spirit glided peacefully, full of sweetness for mortals. Hypnos made humans fall asleep by simply touching them with his magic wand or with a brush of his wings. He could also use his powers on the gods, such as the time when Homer tells how he sent Zeus to sleep, in the form of a night bird. He had several children, of which *Morpheus*, the god of dreams, is particularly relevant. On occasion, he was represented as a sleeping youth, with his arm resting on a fallen lamp. His attributes are the horn and the sleeper. His brother Thanatos lived in the Underworld, where their mother, Nyx, had given birth to them. There are no specific legends about him known, but we do know that, rather than being death itself, he was considered its messenger.

For the Romans, Hypnos was called *Somnus*, the god of sleep, and his twin brother was *Mors*, the god of death. The sons of Night lived in a cave in a peaceful and remote valley of the shadowy realms of Pluto, which was reached by the river Lethe. Near the entrance of the cave, dark forms were always watching, disturbing carpets of poppies, and with their fingers to their lips, imposing silence on whoever entered. The spirits of sleep and death were represented in the art world with crowns of poppies and sometimes bearing a funeral urn or an inverted torch.

Their cave was divided into chambers, each darker and quieter than the last. In one of these internal rooms, behind black curtains, was the soft bed on which Somnus reclined. The king of dreams wore black robes decorated with golden stars and a crown of poppies, and he held a goblet filled with the flowers. His lethargic head was supported by Morpheus, who acted as his principal minister and was in charge of watching over his long slumber and his profound dreams, impeding anybody who tried to disturb him. In the same chamber, there mixed a multitude of delicate spirits, the Dreams, with the terrible Nightmares. They were frequently sent to earth, under the watch of Mercury, to visit the humans while they slept.

There were two doors that led to the valley of dreams, one of ivory, through which illusory dreams passed, and the other of horn, which was the gateway for dreams that were to become reality. This was also the door for dreams that were to prepare men for ill-fortune.

Mors occupied one of the corners in Somnus' cave. He was dressed in a flowing shroud and held a sandglass and a scythe in his hands. He was a horrible, ghastly god, with lifeless sunken eyes, always fixed on the sands of time. When the sand ran out, he knew somebody's life had reached its end, and he went swiftly, with his scythe, to take his prey with merciless enjoyment. The Romans were terrified of Mors and dedicated to him neither cult nor homage. Persephone was worshipped in his place, as a more pleasant and beautiful emblem of death. The Greek "lacedemons" gave him the most attention and always placed their statues together.

Morpheus, the son and adviser of Somnus, was also considered the god of sleep, and mortals were accustomed to ask for his virtuous intervention. He was represented as a winged sleeping child, with a goblet in one hand and poppies in the other, which he shook vigorously to provoke a state of somnolence.

The *Ceres* were also Nyx's daughters. They were spirits

of death, and their appearance was monstrous and horrific. Their bodies were covered by a blanket of blood, and they had long sharp teeth and powerful black wings. They swooped above the wounded that had fallen in battle and sucked their blood, until the last drop. In *The Iliad*, the Ceres differ from the Moirae in that they personify the different destinies that the hero must choose forever. Much later, the Ceres appear as evil spirits that advise the men to commit evil deeds.

The *Sirens* also belong to this group of evil female spirits. Originally they were monsters with the body and legs of a bird and the head of a woman, which lived on the coasts and attracted sailors to their deaths with their melodious singing. Greek and Roman authors did not agree about the origins of these marine divinities. It is supposed that they lived in western Sicily and that they were the daughters of Achelous and Terpsichore, Melpomene, or Phorcys. Only two heroes were able to resist their fatal charms: Orpheus and Ulysses. However, a wise man worked out that by extracting the spell from their singing they would die, and enraged by the resistance of Ulysses and Orpheus, they were hurled out to sea, where they were converted into stone. With the passing of time, they came to be seen as beautiful and harmless beings, with the head and body of a woman and the tail of a fish.

The *Harpies* were the daughters of Thaumas and the Oceanid Electra, and were called *Aello, Okypete,* and *Kelaeno.* According to Hesiod, they were winged women with beautiful flowing hair. Little by little, legend turned them into horrible monsters, with the form of bony vultures, with wrinkled faces and curved beak and talons, surrounded by a putrid odour. Their appearance was the manifestation of drought, hunger, or plague, for their appetites were insatiable. They took children and drove the dead to the reign of Hades. The gods were unwilling to destroy them, because their evil could be used to torment humans, such as in the story of the blind man Phineas, whose food they constantly stole or spoiled. The Harpies were expelled by the sons of Boreas, *Zetes* and *Calais*, who took up residence on the Strophades islands. However, their evil deeds continued, and the Romans often assimilated them with the *Furies*, the guardians of the land of Tartarus.

To the Romans, the Furies were demons from the Underworld, and although they were inspired by Etruscan infernal divinities, they had a very important place in religion. According to some authors, the Furies took their name, origins and cult from the three Greek Erinyes and were the spiritual avengers of Justice, which punished crimes between family members.

The three *Erinyes* were called *Alecto*, *Tisiphone*, and *Megaera*, and they had wings and hair of snakes. They had a whip in one hand and a torch in the other, to administer the punishments of the gods and torment guilty humans. To explain their origins, Hesiod said they were born from the blood of the mutilated Uranus when it fell to the Earth. Aeschylus told that they were the daughters of the River Acheron, who had mated with Night. They were older than Zeus himself and lived in the Erebus. Their tasks consisted of listening to the complaints of humans about the bad treatment of the young to the old, parents to their children, and hosts to their guests, as well as punishing such crimes by ceaselessly tormenting the wrongdoers. It was considered unwise to mention them in conversation, so they often were referred to as the *Eumenides*, which means 'the good-hearted'.

The most important and well-known of the Erinyes was the youngest sister, *Megaera*, which means 'Hate'. She had two main functions: to stir up anger, envy, rage, and jealousy amongst humans and to drive them to bloody confrontation, rape, and other such crimes. In the Underworld she devoted herself, along with her sisters, to tormenting criminals, whom she herself had often impelled to commit their crimes. Like the Erinyes, *Mania* also had the power to drive humans mad and push them into committing acts of violence or sacrilege. This divinity represented Madness.

The *Gorgons* were three sisters: *Euryale, Stheno,* and *Medusa*, the daughters of Phorcys and his sister Ceto, the children of Gaea and Pontus. They lived near the Kingdom of Darkness, in a place unknown to all. Their appearance was terrifying: they had huge heads, with hair of snakes and teeth as long as the tusks of a wild boar, and they flapped through the air on golden wings. They had the power to turn anyone who looked upon them to stone. Only Medusa, the most powerful of the three, was mortal, and she inspired particular terror in humans. There are several myths that offer an explanation of the deeds of these creatures. One tells that Medusa was really a beautiful woman who was too proud of her beauty and flowing hair. It was then that Poseidon fell in love and seduced her. Athena punished the arrogance and pride of Medusa by converting her mane of hair into hideous snakes and making her face horribly ugly. The story of her death also has several versions. Before she died, she had two sons by Poseidon, *Pegasus* and *Chrysaor*.

Her sisters were called the *Graeae*, which means 'old'. They were also three: *Pephredo*, *Enyo,* and *Deino*. The three were ancient and decrepit women who shared one eye and one tooth between the three of them, so that, while one was using them, the other two slept. Their mission was to guard the path that led to their sisters' house.

Though he was not considered a deity, we should also mention *Cerberus*, who was born of the union of two monsters, Typhon and Echidna, and who was the faithful guardian of the entrance to the Underworld. He was a three-headed dog with snakes for a tail, and his bite was as poisonous as a viper. He stood in a cavern on the shores of the Styx and allowed the dead souls to enter the Underworld, but permitted nobody to leave. The fearful mortals who even tried to approach the entrance were cruelly ripped apart in his jaws. However, he was fooled on a number of occasions, such as by Psyche or Deiphobe with cakes or Orpheus with music. Hercules also defeated him in a fight with just his bear hands, which was a great humiliation for the terrible dog.

In Rome, there were other gods related to evil or to death, such as *Consus*, a divinity whose origins are as remote as they are mysterious. He was considered a god of the Underworld, because his alter was found buried in the middle of the Circus Maximus in Rome. It is supposed that his mission was to protect the cereal sown or buried in the earth from the cold and harmful elements.

Laverne was another Roman deity of mysterious origin, who frequented places of ill-repute and granted immunity to bandits who invoked her. She was therefore the goddess of thieves.

Lara, sometimes called 'Muta' or 'Tacita', was considered by the Romans as the goddess of silence and was the heroine of a myth told by Ovid in his work *Fasti*. According to the myth, she was a naiad who was as famous for her beauty as she was for her incessant talking. The naiad, a nymph of Almon, a stream that flowed into the Tiber, dared to disobey the orders of Jupiter. The great god, who had fallen in love with Juturna, asked for help from all the nymphs of the area. Lara not only refused to help, but ran to Juno and revealed Jupiter's intentions to her. To punish her, and to prevent future gossip in Olympus, Jupiter tore out her tongue and exiled her to the Underworld. Mercury was charged with taking her to Hades, but on their way, the messenger god succumbed to her beauty, which without her incessant chattering, made her enchanting and irresistible. He seduced her, and she gave birth to *Lares*. However, the Romans considered Lara the goddess of inefficiency and one of the divinities of eternal silence, a representation of death.

6. HECATE, THE GREAT GODDESS OF MAGIC

Hecate was the daughter of Perseus and Asteria, which makes her from the first generation of gods. Thus when the children of Cronus reigned under the supreme authority of Zeus, the goddess maintained her prior privileges and prerogatives. In ancient times, she was considered a goddess of good deeds, the distributor of material and spiritual riches, and of victory, both to mortals and the immortal gods, who respected and feared her.

Thus Hecate acquired a terrible and wicked character. She was supposed to be the messenger of demons and ghosts, and it was said that she was always accompanied by her faithful dog and a noisy pack of hounds. The Greeks made her the great goddess of magic, who was found at crossroads, where she devoted herself to the arts of magic and prediction. For this reason, her statue was erected on crossroads, and travellers left sacrifices at her feet in the hope of obtaining her favours through magic spells.

She was represented as a divinity with three heads and was sometimes related to Selene, Artemis, and Persephone. It was she who helped Demeter in her search for her daughter, and who later became Persephone's preferred companion, when she was fated to live in the Underworld. Medea became her priestess, and she was also considered the goddess of witches.

7. THE GODDESSES OF DESTINY

It is possible no other idea has such an important place in religion, in tragedy, or in Greek mythology, for both humans and gods, as the complex notion of destiny. To the Greeks, destiny was represented by the Moirae, Tyche, and Nemesis.

The Moirae were the masters of human fate. At first, they were one divinity, but she became so important that she was split into three sisters: *Clotho, Lachesis,* and *Atropos*, who was the smallest and the most feared. Their presence in the Greek cult is as ancient as the very beginnings of religion and myth, as they were supposed to be the daughters of Erebus and Nyx, or of Zeus and Themis. The Moirae lived in a palace near Olympus, where they watched over the evolution of all humans. Zeus weighed up the lives of the humans and informed the Moirae of his decisions, although they could differ in opinion and save those who they chose. Clotho spun thread, and her spinning wheel symbolised the course of existence; Lachesis measured the thread with her wand, which symbolised the fortune reserved for each individual; and Atropos would cut, with no mercy, the thread of life.

Over the centuries, the Greeks softened this notion of cruel destiny and worshipped another god, *Tyche*, who was less terrible and personified chance, both good and bad, just or unjust. In order to obtain her protection, each city built a temple in her honour and erected a statue of her image. In general, she was represented as a powerful woman surrounded by her various attributes (a horn of abundance or a ship's wheel), which turned toward uncertain destinies, be they god or bad.

Tyche was the daughter of Zeus, who granted her the power of deciding the fate of humanity. She was totally irresponsible and unjust in her decisions: to some she conceded the horn of abundance, and from others she took away all they possessed. She ran around with juggling balls to demonstrate the uncertainty of fate. But if a human who had been blessed by Tyche and the horn of abundance failed to sacrifice some of his profits to the gods or to share his fortune with fellow citizens, *Nemesis*, the old goddess of revenge, would appear to punish him. Nemesis had an apple branch in one hand and a wheel in the other. She wore a crown adorned with crows, and a whip was curled at her waist.

Nemesis was a primitive goddess of Attica and, little by little, came to be worshipped in Greece. Her revenge was never blind, like the decisions of Tyche, she simply watched over the proud mortal race so they did not come to believe themselves the equals of the gods. Thus she protected the cosmic order. She punished those who had become proud at receiving too many gifts and advised Tyche on moderation and humans on discretion. Nemesis was also represented with her index finger to her lips.

According to some authors, *Themis*, 'The Equity', the daughter of Titans Uranus and Gaea, bore the Horae, the Moirae, the nymphs of the Eridanus, and some even believe the Hesperides as well. Homer wrote that Themis was the personification of established order and the laws that governed justice. She was respected by all the other gods and often attended the debates of both gods and mortals, to preserve the equity of any decisions taken.

On occasion, she was defined as the divinity who had the gift of prophecy and who supposedly substituted as Gaea's oracle at Delphi before Apollo took over the role. She was represented with a set of scales and a sword, symbol of justice. But her covered eyes were seen as the symbol of her impartiality over the judgments she made.

In fact, the Romans identified her with their own goddess *Justice*, who had a severe and dignified presence and was supposed to have inhabited the Earth when humanity still lived in peace and were unfamiliar with evil. But after the Golden Age, when wickedness and ambition evolved in the heart of humanity, the goddess fled from the Earth and hid herself in the skies, where she is said to have become the constellation Libra.

We also can include Pluto, the god of abundance and son of Iasion and Demeter, who met at Cadmus and Harmony's wedding and made love three times in a ploughed field. Pluto was the result of this union and was the personification of wealth. It was said that in order to prevent the same thing happening with Tyche, Zeus denied her the gift of sight, so that she would dispense her gifts with no account of whether the beneficiary was rich or poor. According to the Romans, Pluto was abandoned as a child and brought up by Pax, the god of peace, who is usually represented with the baby in her arms. When he saw that Pluto only bestowed his gifts on noble and good mortals, Zeus took away his sight so that the god's choices for his gifts would be indiscriminate.

The Romans called the Moirae *Parcas*, and individually *Nona, Decuma*, and *Morta*. They resembled the three weavers that in ancient Roman religion represented the three eras of life: birth, marriage, and death. They were also called the 'Tria Fata', of 'the three fates', feared images of Fatum (Destiny), to whom all life was linked. There are also authors who hold, as Pythia confessed in an oracle, that Jupiter himself was at the mercy of the Moirae, as they were the daughters of the great goddess *Necessity*, against whom even the gods dared not stand and who was known as the 'Great Destiny'.

The Roman people were more superstitious than the Greeks. To them 'Fatum' had a more abstract, less personal character. It was somewhat intangible, as the translation of divine will that reached humans through oracles and others and against which humans could do nothing but follow. It represented total submission to supreme judgment. In time, thanks to the Greek influence, the Roman people gradually humanised the notion of Fatum, dividing it into two entities: *Fatus* for men and *Fata* for woman. In their new roles, these spirits followed the mortals and were trusted by them, watching over their daily lives.

Aside from these spirits, the Romans also worshipped *Fortuna* as the Greeks worshipped Tyche, as the personification of chance, arbitrary and whimsical in her judgments and favours. Fortuna was the most feared of the Roman gods, and her oracles were heeded with reverential terror. Her most famous sanctuaries were in Antius and Preneste. The goddess of chance and fortune presided over all events and was an omnipotent force. The fate of all humans depended on the whim of the great goddess. She was invoked as *Fortuna Virilis* by men and *Fortuna Mulieris* by women. She also was called by travellers, knights, and anyone who performed a task that could be uncertain or dangerous.

Fortune was represented as a powerful woman, holding the horn of abundance and a ship's wheel, for she guided the course of events, and her face was concealed by a veil, showing that the destiny she offered to humanity was neither studied nor premeditated.

8. ERIS, DISCORD, AND HER DAUGHTERS ATE AND LETHE

Eris, or Discord, was the daughter of Nyx, the Night, but she also was considered the twin sister of Ares, the god of war. It was said that she was conceived by Hera when she touched a certain flower. Eris would accompany her brother into battle and rouse hate between the soldiers. Not much more is known about Eris, except for the fundamental role she played in the Trojan War.

The Judgment of Paris

It happened that everybody was invited to the wedding of Tethys and Peleus except Eris, who in revenge threw a golden apple bearing the inscription "for the most beautiful" onto the table where Hera, Aphrodite, and Athena were seated. Zeus refused to act as judge in the matter, as the participants were his wife and daughters, and thus the mortal Paris was chosen to make the judgment. The Trojan was bribed by the goddesses, who attempted to seduce him with magnificent presents. Hera offered him the kingdom of Asia, Athena the glory of war and high victory, and Aphrodite tempted him with the love of Helen, the most beautiful woman in Greece.

The frivolous Paris preferred to choose his love for Helen over power or glory and awarded the golden apple to Aphrodite, the goddess of love and, from then on, also the goddess of beauty. But he engendered a ferocious hate on the part of Hera and Athena toward him and all his people, and their vengeance was the beginning of the great Trojan War.

* * *

Eris gave birth to a series of unfortunate and abstract divinities, such as Hunger, Sorrow, and Forgetfulness. Out of all of them Ate and Lethe were the most important. *Ate*, one of the numerous allegorical mythological divinities, was the daughter of Eris and Zeus. She personified the confusion between mortals, encouraging them to make mistakes that led to their perdition. The goddess lost the right to live amongst the gods in Olympus when she hindered Zeus' pursuit of the things he desired. Zeus promised to make his future son Hercules the supreme leader of Mycenae, but Hera, who was following Ate's advice, made sure that Perseus' other descendant Euristeus was born first, taking the right to the empire that Zeus had promised his stepbrother. Zeus, fed up with Ate's meddling, picked her up by the hair and hurled her to the Earth, forbidding her to ever set foot in the kingdom of the gods. From then on, she lived with the humans, provoking confusion and mistakes among them.

Lethe was a spring in the Underworld where the souls of the dead went to sate their thirst, and the water made them forget their past suffering and previous terrestrial circumstances. Nobody knows who her father was, only that her mother was Eris. Some believe her to be the mother of the Charities. In time, and under the influence of neo-platonic thought, Lethe became a river from which every soul returning to Earth had to drink, to forget the body that it had left behind and, in particular, to erase the memories of the images of the Underworld and of death. This was another mythological explanation that the Greeks gave to reincarnation or the transmigration of the soul.

9. DIVINITIES OF BEAUTY AND HARMONY

There were three groups of divinities, all daughters of Zeus, who represented beauty and harmony, the ideals pursued by the Ancient Greek way of thought and their supreme conventions of the aesthetic interests.

The *Horae* were born from the union between Zeus and Themis (Equity) and received names that were related to life in society: *Eunomia* (Legality), *Dice* (Justice), and *Irene* (Paz). They were goddesses of vital harmony and balance and creators of well-being and cohabitation. But Dice is the one of most mythological interest.

The goddesses were also called *Thallo, Carpo,* and *Auxo*. They presided over the order of nature and the seasons and, therefore, represented the most habitual traditions. Later, when the Greeks divided the day into twelve Hours, they increased the number of hours. It is difficult to define their attributions, as they do not figure in the legends of Greek mythology or in the ideas concerning how the gods evolved and changed in the course of the Ancient times.

They were represented as three young and happy women, dancing together with the Muses and the Graces and carrying agricultural products from the different seasons: flowers, brambles, vines, and fruit. The cult of the Horae was born in the Silver Age, when people first started to differentiate between the seasons of the year. As time passed they lost their meteorological characteristics and came to represent the order of humanity in nature and its eras or periods: infancy, youth, and maturity, which correspond to the seasons of spring, summer, and autumn. As goddesses of fertility, they made the labours of humans prosperous and were present only in happy times. They were never part of the unhappy eras of humanity.

The *Charities* formed a triad, which according to Hesiod personified both charm and beauty. Ancient traditions and texts, however, are not in agreement about their origins or their parentage. Some believe that they were the daughters of Zeus and Aphrodite, as the Greeks often associated the cult of the goddess of beauty to that of the Charities. But they are considered by others to be the daughters of Lethe, who was the daughter of Eris, Discord. The last theory, which is the most credible and supported by scholars, says the Charities are the daughters of Zeus and Eurynome, the most beautiful Oceanid.

The Charities were called *Aglaia* (Resplendent), *Euphrosyne* (beautiful soul), and *Thalia* (Flourishing), and they personified the blooming of nature. Their principal function was to share out charm, beauty, and warmth, as their names imply. They directed the sun's rays onto the Earth, comforted human hearts, rewarded their lives with happiness, and presided over good social relations.

They lived in Olympus and were great friends of the Muses, as they shared a love of poetry. They were linked with art by their beauty and harmony and have been represented by artists as three beautiful young women who appear naked, with one of them looking in the opposite direction from her companions. One group of statues in Elis gives an idea of their respective attributions: one carries a dart, another a rose, and the last a branch of myrtle. The Romans called these three goddesses the Graces, and together they represented beauty, the enjoyment of which leads to fertility.

The *Muses* are the most important and evolved group of collective gods, which was formed by the nine daughters of Zeus and Mnemosyne (Memory). Although at first they were considered three nymphs who presided over the different forms of poetry, they were raised by popular imagination to the level of Zeus' daughters, and their functions became more independent until they became the group of nine Muses. Their chant made the chorus that accompanied the god of the lyre, Apollo, who was also sometimes called Musageta.

The Muses had numerous homes, which generally corresponded to places of culture or legend. Although they lived in Olympus, where they distracted the other gods with their chants and dances, they also lived in the choicest places on Earth, such as Mount Pierus, named so in memory of the nine daughters of Pierus, the king of Macedonia, who wanted to compete with the Muses and, as a punishment, were turned into starlings by Apollo. They also inhabited Mount Helicon and the sacred streams of Agannipe and Hippocrene, where poets went in search of inspiration.

It is not surprising that their mother was Mnemosyne, the goddess of Memory, a faculty that is related to artistic inspiration, which comes from the past as much as from the present, and sometimes from the future.

The muses are usually represented as beautiful young women, with happy smiling faces, serious or more playful, according to the functions of each goddess, and directly implicated in artistic creation, which also derives from the concept 'beautiful'. And as the arts express diverse manifestations, with time each artistic activity became personalised under the influence of a particular muse.

In Greek culture, the arts are generally grouped under the heading '*corea*', which includes words, whose artistic expression is formed by poetry and literature; sound, with music as the manifestation; and movement, manifested in this sense by dance. With a view to this classification, a number of arts are derived from the names of the nine Muses:

COREA

WORD

CALLIOPE, 'the beautiful voice'. Muse of Heroic and Epic Poetry, she was represented wearing a laurel crown.

ERATO, 'the adorable'. Muse of Lyrical and Erotic Poetry, she was represented with a lyre.

THALIA, 'the festive'. Muse of Comedy and Pastoral Poetry, she was represented with a shepherd's crook and mask, wearing a crown of wild flowers.

MELPOMENE, 'the song-worshipped'. Muse of Tragedy, she wore a golden crown and carried a dagger and a sceptre.

CLIO, 'who gives fame'. Muse of History, she remembered all great and heroic actions and the names of their authors. She was usually represented wearing a laurel crown, with a book and quill, ready to write down all that happened to the mortal humans or the gods.

URANIA, 'the celestial'. Muse of Astronomy and Philosophy, she held mathematical instruments as representation of her love for exact science.

SOUND

POLYHYMNIA, 'of varied hymns'. Muse of Rhetoric and Hymns, she held a sceptre to show that eloquence governed with unopposed dominion.

EUTERPE, 'the charming'. Muse of Music, also called the Lady of the Song, she was represented with a flute and garlanded with fragrant fresh flowers.

MOVEMENT

TERPSICHORE, 'the lover of the dance'. Muse of Dancing, she was represented with her light feet in the middle of an aerial dance step.

10. THE HESPERIDES

The *Hesperides* were the guardians of the famous golden apples and lived in the western confines of the Earth, beyond the Columns of Hercules (the Strait of Gibraltar), where humans dared not go. They were the three daughters of the Titan Atlas and all were young and beautiful, living a carefree life while they watched over the enchanted gardens in which the magic apple tree grew.

They were called *Aegle, Erytheis,* and *Hesperarethusa* and were helped in their task as guardians by *Ladon*, the dragon whose father was Ceto and whose sisters were the Gorgons and the Graeae. According to a second theory, the Hesperides were the daughters of Ceto and Phorcys and, therefore also the sisters of the dragon.

The golden apple tree was the gift given to Hera by Gaea, the Mother Earth, when she married Zeus, and which Hera then put under the care of the Hesperides in the gardens of the goddess in Mount Atlas. On one occasion, the tyrannical king Busiris of Egypt sent his men to capture the Hesperides, whose beauty had made them famous. But Hercules, who was among the king's messengers, annihilated the whole troop. However, one of the twelve tasks set to Hercules was to steal the apples of the tree, which he did by tricking Atlas. Hercules consecrated the apples to Athena and later returned them.

11. THE NYMPHS

The Greeks used this general name to describe all the female divinities of nature that lived in the seas, rivers, fields, forests, mountains, rocks, trees, grottoes, and so on. They were represented by young girls of exceptional beauty, with long flowing hair, who appeared naked or semi-naked. They were a sort of ancient fairy, and they were all considered to be the daughters of Zeus and the Sky, and their birth was given a very poetical description. The god fertilised the Sky, and small drops of rain fell to the Earth, which formed streams, rivers, and the seas, and at the same time gave them life. For this reason, in ancient times, the nymphs had a natural strength that presided over the reproduction and fertility of nature, and which they carried out by mixing with the water, the humidity in the air, and the forests.

However, their good deeds were not only restricted to nature. Humans also benefited from their tender care. Lovers who bathed in the waters of certain streams in order to purify themselves and promote fertility were protected by the nymphs. But apart from the regenerating qualities that were particularly appreciated by the ancient people, the nymphs had two other great powers: the ability to carry out great feats and their love of foresight. They were capable of inspiring noble thoughts in the men that came to taste the sacred waters of their streams. They would also reveal to people the final result of an illness, whether happy or sad.

The nymphs were not immortal beings, but could love for thousands of years and preserve a youthful appearance, carefree and singing in trees over their lakes. Nymphs showed up in many legends, in which they fell in love, not only with the gods, but also with mortals. From these unions were born the heroes, demi-gods, and the ancestors of the first human beings.

Greek mythology classifies the nymphs according to the place they inhabit:

1.– *The Nereids,* nymphs of the sea, were the fifty daughters of Nereus and Doris. They are also considered by some as the nymphs of the Mediterranean.

These marine goddesses live on the sea bed, in a brightly lit palace, where they dance for their father Nereus, the ancient god of the sea, who precedes even Poseidon, and was the son of Gaea and Pontus. However, each nymph personified a form or aspect of the surface of the water, where they often appeared as beautiful mermaids and mixed with the waves and the seaweed, riding the sea horses at the side of the Titans. There are very few legends attributed to these nymphs, but some of them became very well-known. *Amphitrite*, for example, married Poseidon; *Orithyia, Galatea* and *Thetis*, wife of Peleus and mother of Achilles.

2.– *The Naiads*, nymphs of the waters, springs, rivers, and brooks. Legends are not in agreement about to their origins. According to Homer, they were born from Zeus' union with the Sky, though other authors name Oceanus as the father.

The Naiads were young lovely women, with skin as white as the moon, who were constantly desired by both men and gods. But they knew how to defend themselves against unwanted attentions and could drive persisting suitors mad. They sometimes paralysed those who bathed without permission in forbidden or sacred waters. But they also were generous to those who asked for a cure to their sickness and who bathed in waters or streams with healing properties. These beautiful nymphs also were considered the patrons of song and poetry.

3.– *The Dryads,* nymphs of the vegetation, from the oak forests, whose name comes from the Greek 'drus', meaning 'oak'. The forests where these nymphs lived were usually sacred forests in Greek religion, and the nymphs protected their trees from sacrilegious vandals who may cut them down.

The nymphs were fresh and vigorous like the trees they guarded, and each adopted the form and size of her tree and its roots. However, nymphs also left the forests to get married. Eurydice, the most well-known nymph, married Orpheus.

4.– *The Hamadryads* were the nymphs of the forests. Like the dryads, they chose to inhabit the beautiful forests, living in the shelter of their selected tree. But these nymphs gave up their freedom when they inhabited a tree, and the death of the tree would mean the end of their own existence. For this reason, woodcutters took pity on their pleas for mercy when they cut down a tree and did not follow the example of Erysichthon, who took no heed of their pitiful cries and was later harshly punished for his sacrilegious act and his cruel heart.

5.– *The Alseids* were the nymphs of the flowers and hardly any reference to them exists.

6.– *The Oreads* were the nymphs of the mountains, who lived on sparse slopes overlooking their domain. The Oreads were not of the same sweet and gentle character as their cousins of the valleys and forests. They were lovers of risk and of violent pleasures. With Artemis, the goddess of the hunt, they pursued their prey into the most perilous situations, to the edge of sheer cliffs, with no regard for danger or their own spent energy. The Romans believed these nymphs hid themselves in the desolate mountains to follow tired travellers through the rocky labyrinth of pathways.

7.– *The Napaea* lived in the small green valleys that they maintained lush and fruitful with their care. The dryads also helped them in their tasks. The Napaea were renowned for their beauty and inhabited the slopes of the hills, the shaded valleys, and the fertile forests, where they encouraged the cycle of the buds and grasses.

8.– *The Meliads*, on the other hand, only lived in ash trees. These were the nymphs born from the blood that dropped from the wounds of Uranus when he was avenged by his son, Cronus. To commemorate the myth, the Greeks assigned them the ash trees as their home, which in those times were used to make fierce weapons designed to cause the loss of much blood.

The Meliads were responsible for the protection of abandoned nymphs, for which they employed the branches of the ash, whose foliage made a natural shelter from harm. Other legends also attribute the Meliads with the power to protect livestock.

12. THE ASTRAL GODS

Once the ancient peoples had established Zeus as the absolute ruler of Olympus and the god of the Sky, they still had to create a series of atmospheric gods to explain why, for example, the sun rose each morning or the cold North Wind blew. Though the atmospheric powers and the attributes of the astral beings were included in Zeus' range of powers, he is not the father of the 'astral gods'. The most important divinities that personified the main stars were the children of the Titans Theia and Hyperion: Helios (the Sun), Selene (the Moon), and Eos (the Dawn), who were from the first generation of the gods.

Helios was the divine representation of the Sun, the heat and solar light. The idea that Sun was the giver of light and warmth, indispensable to life and the centre of the world and totally opposed to dark and the shadowy world of death, acquired considerable importance toward the end of Antiquity, to the point that the Sun god was converted into the essential god, under various denominations such as Mitra, Sol Sanctissimus, Sol Invictus, and Heliogabalus, or even, near the end of Paganism, the only god. But Helios was not among the great Greek gods and only achieved a modest position in the Greek pantheon, where he soon was assimilated with Apollo.

Above all, Helios was Zeus' servant, and everyday he mounted his golden chariot to guide him through the skies. He wore a golden helmet and a cape that blew in the wind. The four steeds that drew his chariot of fire were magnificent glittering beasts, harnessed also in gold, and they bore the light and heat from one extreme of the Earth to the other and, with it, the germination of all life.

Helios' first union was with *Perseis*, with whom he had several children that would later have an important role in many legends, including Aeetes, who travelled with the Argonauts, and *Pasiphae*, who was the wife of King Minus of Crete. He also had seven sons with the nymph *Rhode*, daughter of Poseidon and Halia, including *Actis*, who founded the city of Heliopolis in Egypt and was the first to teach astrology to the Egyptians, inspired by his father Helios. It was in Rhodes where the Colossus – one of the Seven Wonders of the World – was built, seventy feet high, in honour of the Sun god. It was lost in an earthquake. Helios had seven daughters with the Oceanid *Clymene*, called the *Heliadae*, and one son *Phaeton*, who was the hero of a Greek legend that tells of the danger of natural disasters.

The legend of Phaeton

It is told that Phaeton, who resided in Ethiopia, heard that the son of Io and Zeus, Epaphus, was spreading doubts about his divine ancestry. Thus he went to his father's palace to ask for some proof of the truth. Helios swore on the River Styx that he was indeed Phaeton's father, and as proof he promised to give him anything he asked for. The fearful Phaeton asked that he may be allowed to drive the chariot of fire for one day. Faced with the insistence of his son and the binding of his own promise, Helios was forced to agree to Phaeton's request, and after advising him on how to handle the horses, he handed over the reigns. But the horses were nervous, and when they found themselves in the inexpert hands of a new driver, they bolted and bore the Sun on an erratic course that carried it so far from the Earth, all the people began to shiver. Then, they swooped down so close to the surface, all the rivers and lakes dried up. Zeus struck Phaeton down with a great bolt of lightning, and he fell into the River Po and the sun chariot returned to its course.

The Phaeton's three sisters, the Heliadae, called *Lampetia*, *Phaethousa,* and *Phoebe*, cried for four months over the remains of their brother at the shore of the river (some say it was the River Eridanus). The gods sympathised with such great pain and converted the sisters into white maple trees, and their tears turned into beads of amber. The amber, which shone with a profound beauty, resembled the colour of the sun's rays and the transparency of a tear. This legend gave the stone the mythical justification that favoured its trade.

* * *

Helios was a man of splendid beauty, and on his brow he wore a crown of golden rays. Legend tells us that he was woken by the cock's crow and his sister Eos' call, and how he drove his golden chariot from his palace in the Far East, near to Colchis, to his second palace, as magnificent as the first, in the Far West, where the four splendid horses grazed on the Islands of the Fortunate. He returned home on the ocean's current, the horses and chariot borne on a golden platform.

Helios was the only god who could view the entire face of the Earth in one gaze and inform the other gods of Olympus of what was happening. In this function, he appears in many legends, be it to warn Hephaestus that Aphrodite was cheating on him with Ares, or informing Demeter that her daughter's kidnapper was no other than Hades. But he was not always such a good watchman, as on one occasion he did not realise that Ulysses and his men were stealing his flock.

Selene is the personification of the moon, and she shone with great intensity in the Greek skies. The Moon goddess slept while her brother Helios crossed the skies in his golden chariot, and when he reached the end of his journey, she took up the reigns of her black horses and flew out in her silver carriage to follow the same course her brother had set, under the protection of the bright stars and the blanket of night.

After Aphrodite, the goddess of the Moon was the most desired goddess. Her lovers were very numerous, and her best-known affairs were with Zeus and, later, Pan, who seduced her by concealing himself under white robes. But her most famous passionate encounter was with the handsome shepherd *Endymion*, who was king of the Aetolians. Together they had fifty daughters.

On one occasion, Endymion asked the gods to grant him immortality in return for remaining deeply asleep for the rest of eternity. Zeus granted his desire and sent Endymion into a profound slumber that permitted him, in his dreams, to stay young and handsome forever. From then on, Selene visited her unconscious lover each night, where he rested in a cold cave, and she caressed him with rays of silver, uniting the two without waking him or disturbing the peace of his slumber. Selene was said to be so beautiful, with perfect white skin, that when she drove her carriage into the silver sky, she was the most beautiful of all the stars. Legend also tells that each eclipse was due to a dragon that prepared to devour her. But the wizards of Thessaly were charged with

Aphrodite and Eros.

frightening the monster and stop it from carrying out its macabre intentions.

The legends of Selene, which are few, are always related to her love affairs, as she travelled the skies each night in search of lovers, who she kept entertained with kisses and caresses until dawn. This mythical attribution has been taken up by many romantic poets, suffering from the pains of love, and thus the word *luna* acquired romantic and sad implications, imposing 'lunacy' on its sufferers.

Eos, the youngest sister of these divinities, was the divine personification of the Dawn in Greek mythology. When the night came to its end and Selene returned to her magnificent palace to rest, Eos arose in the East, mounted her golden chariot, and drove to Olympus, where she announced the arrival of the morning to Helios. When he appeared, she would accompany him on his journey until she saw him safe and sound to the western shores of the great ocean.

Eos had several lovers and husbands and a large number of children. But her official husband was *Astraeus*, the Evening Wind, a descendant of the Titans, with whom she had the Morning Star, the winds and the other stars. On one occasion, Aphrodite caught in Eos Ares' bed, and Aphrodite put a curse on her that she would constantly be attracted to young mortals. From then on, Eos began to seduce several mortals in secret and shame, such as Orion, a handsome hunter from Hyria and the son of Poseidon and Euriale. And later, she seduced Cephalus and then Clitus. Finally, she kidnapped Ganymede and Tithonus, the sons of Tros. But Zeus had been struck by Ganymede's beauty as well and took him from her. So she asked Zeus to grant Tithonus immortality, as compensation, and he granted her wish. But Eos had forgotten a small, though important, detail: she should have asked for eternal youth along with immortality. Thus the handsome young man became older and older: his voice wavered, and his skin became wrinkled and dry. When Eos grew tired of caring for him, he became a pile of ash.

Popular legend characterises Eos as the goddess who kidnapped men at dawn, with whom she fell irremediably in love, due to Aphrodite's curse. In this way, the Greeks explain the sudden release that lovers experience at the first light of dawn.

The Morning Star, daughter of Eos and Astraeus, was given the name *Phosphorous*, or Lucifer by the Romans. The morning star becomes a twilight star in the evening and then receives the name of *Hesperus*. According to legend, Hesperus disappeared from the world of mortals, and it was believed that she had been transformed into the first star that shines at the fall of dusk: the evening star. In both cases, the star is related with the star of Venus.

Zeus took *Iris* as the messenger of his divine will. The winged goddess of eternal youth was the daughter of Thaumas and Electra. She was the messenger and servant of Zeus, and even the confidante of Hera, and she devoted herself to satisfying even the most insignificant wish of her master. Iris symbolised the rainbow, for she personified the marvellous multicoloured bridge between the sky and the Earth, the link between gods and humans that she used in her labour. She took the form of a winged woman who carried the herald's wand in her hand. In later poems, Iris is presented as the wife of Zephyr, the East Wind and the mother of Eros.

The lord of the winds and storms was called *Aeolus* and was the son of Poseidon. His power was not strong, as Zeus had delegated it to him and ordered that all the winds submit to Aeolus. He was charged with controlling the different winds according to the missions commanded by the supreme god. In this way, Zeus commanded him to follow his orders to liberate the winds that were imprisoned within the deep caves of a group of floating islands, called the Aeolian Islands. It is thus no surprise that sailors would invoke Aeolus and make him sacrifices and offerings when they needed favourable winds for their voyage.

If Aeolus ever disobeyed Zeus and liberated the elements for his own pleasure or without the strict control of Zeus, he could release disasters, fierce storms, and shipwrecks. The evil winds destroyed everything in their path and caused all kinds of calamities. The people of Athens worshipped eight winds and built an octagonal temple with the image of the winds in the eight corners, each facing the direction from which it blew.

The winds were more divine powers than gods, but they

were widely venerated by the Greeks. This is easy to explain in a country where nature and agriculture are dependent on the weather that the winds bring to them and where they have an important and prestigious role in the economy.

Apart from the evil winds, there were four main good winds: the *Notos* or Auster (to the Romans), which came from the south and was a warm humid wind; the *Euros* or Volturnus, which came from the Southwest; *Zephyr*, or Favonius in Latin, which came from the east; and *Boreas*, or Alquilo, the harsh north wind. Not much is known about these winds, as only references to the last two have been found in classic mythology.

Zephyr was the personification of the East Wind, which brought freshness and welcomed rains and, therefore, was considered a beneficial wind for the agricultural people. He was represented as a young, winged man, who swooped gently through the sky declaring the wet spring and was a soft breeze that carried the sweet fragrance of flowers. But like the vast majority of the gods, Zephyr had a bad side to his character. One day he saw the handsome Hyacinth with Apollo, and he was overtaken by such a strong attack of jealousy that he killed Hyacinth.

Zephyr was married to the nymph *Cloris*, and they had a son *Carpo*, the fruit. Legend tells that Zephyr granted his wife powers over the flowers of spring and made her the goddess of spring blossom. Cloris was exceptionally beautiful and was always accompanied by her husband.

Boreas was said to have a character equal to the bitter and cold wind that he blew about the Greek lands. He was given the image of an old, bearded man, with wings sprouting from his shoulders and dressed only in a short tunic. It is believed that his winds originated in Thrace, where he inhabited a cavern in Mount Hemo. His legend tells that he kidnapped *Orithyia*, the daughter of Erecteus, king of Athens, wrapped up in a blanket of dark clouds and dust. He forced her to marry him, and she gave birth to many of his children, including two sons, Zetes and Calais, who grew wings when they reached puberty, and two daughters, Chione and Cleopatra. In time, Orithyia became the fresh breeze that cooled the burning air of Greek summers.

172

Caurus, the northwest wind, drove the snow clouds before him.

13. STYX AND HER CHILDREN

Styx was a nymph from the first generation of gods, daughter of Tethys and Oceanus, and she lived in Arcadia, in a grotto next to a stream. She married *Pallas*, and they had four children.

When Zeus and Cronus announced war on each other, Styx decided to take the side of Zeus and took all her children to Olympus, to give them into service of the celestial gods and their just cause. Zeus conceded his brave warriors and helpers the right to remain always at his side and to assist him in future tasks. He also granted Styx, in thanks for her help, the privilege of being invoked whenever the gods swore an oath, which they would swear to Styx, giving her an absolute and sacred role and value.

Thus, when a god wanted to swear an oath, Iris went to the river Styx and filled a goblet, over which the goddess would extend her hand and pronounce the oath heard. The failure to fulfil a promise or an oath made in this way was punishable by a severe chastisement, which could be the deprivation of divine powers, a deep sleep for many years, or sometimes the deity in question could be forbidden from eating ambrosia or drinking nectar, the food and drink of the gods, and moreover, expelled from the circle of the gods for nine years.

In time, Styx became the principal river of the underworld, her muddy and frozen waters flowed through the shadows, and her course wound around the borders of the shadowy realm. The river was born in a sparse and isolated place, and its waters, black and corrosive, flowed into the depths of the earth, confirming the legends that give it its infernal, evil, and perilous characteristics.

Her four sons were *Zelos*, 'Glory' to some and 'Incarnation' to others; *Bia* 'Violence'; *Cratos* 'Force' or 'Power'; and *Nike* 'Victory', which was also one of Athena's names. In the acropolis of Athens a famous temple was built in her

173

honour. She always was associated with Athena, who then received the name Athena Nike. In general, Nike was represented as a winged woman, who carried a palm branch and a crown and guided heroes and gods in the course of their actions. To the Romans, Nike was Victory, and was, therefore, very important. She was always at Jupiter's side, to swiftly carry out any order he may give her. The Romans believed that the effigy of Victory had been created by Palatine, the eponymous hero of the Palatine hill, where he had a temple built in her honour.

14. GAEA AND HER CHILDREN

Gaea was the Mother Earth and part of the primordial triad, according to Hesiod's Theogony. According to different authors, Gaea either was created out of the nothingness or from the union between Aether, Hemera, and Eros. Gaea symbolised the earth as it was being formed, the vengeance and the violence of natural instinct, and the softness and maternal love of the first primitive lands. Moreover, she was the original fertilising element of all things and the protector of all living beings. She was worshipped as a protecting and fertilising goddess, an attribute that was increased by her many children and the multiplication of the human race. Gaea was primarily Mother Earth, the Great Mother, both for gods and humans, for she was the beginning of life. However, though at first she was a highly important divinity, and her meddling in different legends was constant, she was later substituted by other goddesses, such as Demeter or Cybele.

Apart from the children she had with Uranus, the Titans, the Hecatoncheires, and the Cyclops, she also had Pontus, 'wave', Nereus, Thaumas, Ceto, and Phorcys, to name the most well-known.

Nereus was a very ancient sea god, who reigned long before Poseidon, and unlike his follower, was a just, wise, and tranquil god. He married the Oceanid Doris, and together they had the fifty Nereids. He was represented as an old man, with hair and beard as white as the ocean spray. His empire extended over the Aegean Sea, and he lived in a splendid grotto on the ocean bed. But he often left his home to show himself to the humans and predict the future for them.

Thaumas, like the other primitive gods, has no legends of his own. He is known, apart from being of the main branch of primordial sea gods, for engendering with Electra the monstrous Harpies and Iris, the winged messenger of Olympus.

Ceto and *Phorcys* also united and created a great number of the monsters that appear in Greek legends: *Scylla*, the Gorgons, *Echidna*, and the Hesperides and according to other authors: the Gorgons, the Graeae, the dragon Ladon, and the Hesperides.

According to some mythologists, *Echidna* was the daughter of Gaea and Pontus and was a terrible monster – half serpent, half woman. Legend tells that after Echidna lay with *Typhon*, she gave birth to a series of fantastic creatures that were to develop an important role in Greek mythology: *Chimaera*, the dog *Geryon*, *Orthrus*, Cerberus (the guardian of the Underworld), the *Sphinx*, the *Hydra of Lerna*, the dragons of Colchis, *Medusa*, the lion of Nerea, and the eagle that devoured Prometheus' intestines. Her own fertility converted her into a dangerous and evil being that devoured innocent travellers. Argos, the giant of a hundred eyes, killed her when she was sleeping.

Gaea also had other lovers amongst the gods, including Tartarus, with whom she had the fearsome *Typhon*, the most feared monster that ever existed. Legend tells that he was engendered in order to wreak revenge on Zeus for imprisoning the Titans when he defeated them in the war of the Titans. His body was covered in scales, and he had a hundred tongues. Fire and burning rocks spewed from his mouth. It was said that when they saw his ass's head, the writhing serpents in place of arms, and his enormous size, the gods fled to Egypt in terror. Only Athena and Zeus dared to face the monster, whom they defeated after numerous bloody battles.

This fight symbolises the volcanic cataclysm that flattened the Cyclade Islands, leaving the Greeks with no more than a frightening memory. The defeated Typhon also signifies the last anarchic force directed against the law and order of Olympus. However, before he was thrown to the underworld for eternity, he lay with Echidna and produced the fearsome offspring of future legends.

15. THE DESCENDANTS OF POSEIDON

From his legitimate union with the Nereid Amphitrite, Poseidon only had one son, *Triton*. Triton, who was not of Greek origin, was worshipped by sailors and fishermen. He had various aspects, but he was normally represented as having the torso of a man and the tail of a fish. He could be both benevolent and terrible. From his shell, where he lived at the bottom of the sea, he could blow up fearsome storms and tempests. He was worshipped, therefore, as the god who calmed turbulent waters and as an intermediary between Poseidon and the people.

Poseidon had many affairs with goddesses, nymphs, mortals, and even with monsters like Medusa, from which union were born evil and frightening creatures such as the *Cercopes*, the Aloads, *Chrysaor* or the Cyclops Polyphemus. A second theory claims the Cercopes, malicious and evil-doing gnomes, were the offspring of Theia.

The *Aloads* were the two daughters that Poseidon had with Iphimedia, called *Ephialtes* and *Otus*. Both were incredibly tall and uncommonly strong, and legend tells us that they both fell in love with Hera and Aphrodite and decided to kidnap them. To reach the home of the gods, they put Mount Pelion on top of Mount Ossa. But their plan was foiled when they met the poisoned arrows of Apollo, who was furious at their presence there. Once in the Underworld, they received an exemplary punishment: they were tied to a column of snakes while an owl flew gloomily around them.

Antheus was the son Poseidon had with Gaea. He was a monstrous giant that lived in the Libyan Desert and ate lions. His legend tells that he promised his father he would build a temple made of human skulls. To carry out this sinister plan, he would attack any traveller that crossed his path and kill them mercilessly.

The *Telchines* were also believed to be the descendants

of Poseidon, though another theory says they were the sea god's teachers. They were geniuses who were generally bad tempered and were half man, half fish – a form they swapped on occasion for the form of a serpent. They lived on the island of Rhodes, which became the object of their evil deeds. The Greeks attributed most of the calamities suffered by the island to them, such as the rain, snow, or hail. They were even accused of having tipped sulphur into the Styx and of a failed attempt to kill all humans and animals and leave the fertile lands barren. In the end, Zeus had enough of their wickedness and threw them into the sea, where they became huge rocks.

Polyphemus was the giant son of Poseidon and the nymph Thoosa, who lived in a spacious cave near Mount Etna and watched over a flock of fat sheep and woolly lambs. Polyphemus was a Cyclops who had only one eye in the centre of his forehead (*Kyklos* means 'circle', and *ops* means 'gaze'). His legend tells how he fell in love with Galatea, the daughter of Doris and Nereus. But his ugly appearance was such that he frightened the beautiful Nereid, who was already madly in love with Acis, a young shepherd. When he realised his love was unrequited, the monster took revenge on the two lovers by killing them. But the Cyclops is best-known for his part in the legend of Ulysses.

16. THE CENTAURS

The *Centaurs* were born from the union between Ixion and Nephele, the cloud created by Zeus with the appearance of Hera. They had the head and torso of humans, and from the waist down they were horses. They were wild animals that lived on raw meat and inhabited the forests of Thessaly. Their customs were brutal and even dangerous. When the centaurs were intoxicated with wine, they became excited and unpredictable. They were especially feared by women, as they were often targeted by the sexual appetite of the centaurs. But not all centaurs were the same. Some had long hair and manes; others were wise old creatures or young joyful colts, though they all had the strong arm and chest muscles needed to capture young nymphs. Only two centaurs are known to have stood out from the others for their good nature and wisdom, *Chiron* and *Pholus*.

Chiron was the wise centaur that instructed the heroes. He played the lyre, was an expert hunter, a talented healer, and an excellent teacher. Among his famous pupils were Achilles, Jason, and Sculapius. He was wounded accidentally by a poisoned arrow shot by Hercules, and he offered his life in return for Prometheus' pardon, thus freeing himself from eternal and terrible punishment.

On one occasion, it occurred to Pirithous, the king of the Lapiths and companion of the centaurs, to invite them to his wedding. At the banquet, the centaurs drank a great deal of wine and tried to rape the new bride, Hippodameia. There followed a huge fight that everybody was dragged into, which ended in the centaurs fleeing from the wedding.

The myths about these beings with the body of horses were adapted, no doubt, from the fact that the Thessalians, skilled horsemen, came to represent the hybrid creatures in the eyes of the Greeks.

17. THE DIOSCURI

Leda, the daughter of King Thestios of Aetolia, married Tyndareus, who came to live in her father's court when he lost the kingdom of Sparta. But although Leda loved her husband, she was seduced by Zeus, who tricked her by turning himself into a swan. Leda had four children: *Castor* and *Clytemnestra*, who were the legitimate children of Tyndareus; and *Polydeuces* and *Helen*, who were Zeus' children.

The brothers, Castor and Polydueces, were given the name the Dioscuri in Greek mythology, as their fraternal love knew no limits, and they were never apart. This fraternal bond is represented in many legends, as well as works of art, in which they are shown holding hands, and often on medallions, with their profiles in relief.

The brothers were born in Sparta, and they symbolised the

The centaurs.

secular rivalry between Laconia and Attica, heading a victorious expedition against Athena, with the aim of freeing their beloved sister Helen, which earned them the pride of Sparta.

Castor was known for his skills as a soldier and horse-breaker. Polydeuces was the best boxer of his time. The brothers also took part in the wild boar hunt of Calydon and accompanied the Argonauts on their quest, during which they used all their natural skills in the service of Jason.

They did everything together, they even fell in love with sisters, Phoebe and Hilaeira, the daughters of King Leucippus, who were promised to the brothers Idas and Lynceus. Castor and Polydeuces kidnapped the sisters, and their intended husbands pursued them in a bloody fight. Polydeuces was only wounded as he was immortal, but Castor was killed. Polydeuces was inconsolable and refused to accept his immortality if Castor could not share it. Polydeuces' love and generosity for his brother moved Zeus, who took pity on his suffering and conceded his wish of sharing with Castor his don of immortality, every other day, in Olympus. Thus not even death was able to separate the brothers, who were blessed with such fortune on the battlefield and none in matters of love. The cult of the Dioscuri extended from Sparta throughout all of Greece.

18. THE ROMAN ALLEGORIES

The allegorical characters, with no genealogy and no myth, are the divine representation of different abstract concepts: moral concepts, such as Virtue; political concepts, like Peace or Victory; social concepts, such as Poverty; and physical concepts, like Health. These allegories appeared late in Roman civilisation, as most Greeks had no knowledge of them. In Rome they gradually multiplied. Statues were erected; cults were dedicated to them; and even temples were built, which emphasised their characteristics and attributes. Today, however, the evidence is badly defined. Here we can see some of the most important and significant:
- *Friendship*. This was honoured as a character in both

Rome and Greece. It was represented as a young woman wearing a dress that she gathered up in one hand and bearing a crown of flowers or twigs of myrtle in the other.

- *Prudence*. This was later identified with Metis, the first wife of Zeus. She was represented as a mature woman with two faces, one looking toward the future and the other into the past.

- *Hope*. Called *Elpis* by the Greeks, this was the gift from the gods that did not escape from Pandora's Box. For this reason, Hope was worshipped in ancient times with special veneration. The Romans called her '*Spes*' and built several temples to her cult. She was given the features of a lovely young woman, holding the folds of her dress in one hand and a newly opened flower in the other.

- *Happiness*. One of the most important Roman allegorical gods, her image was even printed on coins. She was represented as a voluptuous woman and carried Mercury's *Caduceus* and the horn of abundance. The former symbolised health and the latter opulence, both of which were considered indispensable factors of happiness.

- *Health*. There are no personal legends of this divinity. In Greece she was called *Hygia* and was the daughter of Sculapius. The Romans called her *Salus* and erected several temples to her. Not only the Roman people, but the Roman State, the living body of the nation, was under her protection. She symbolised, in this case, public well-being and prosperity, and she was the object of a great festival, held on the same day as the Concordia and the Janus. Salus was represented with the features of a young girl praying at the altar, accompanied by a serpent, the fundamental symbol of the Underworld. Salus was invoked by the sick and even by the State itself, when the situation was serious enough. She was also sometimes represented as the goddess of fortune, with a ship's wheel in her hand.

- *Concord*. She personified the good understanding between family members, citizens and spouses. Her sister was Peace, with whom she was sometimes confused and from whom she borrowed attributes, such as the pomegranate, the symbol of a fertile conjugal union, and the olive branch, the emblem of peace.

- *Peace*. Her cult appeared later and was identified with one of the three Horae, Irene. Her image was a sweet-faced woman, bearing an olive branch and the horn of abundance.

- *Virtue*. She was the symbol of valour and was often represented at the side of *Honour*. The Romans assimilated the divinities by erecting two sanctuaries. In general, she was a proud and austere woman, carrying a lance and a sword.

- *Hunger.* The daughter of Night, Virgil placed her at the gates of the Underworld, bearing sterility to the fields. Ovid described her as a woman kneeling in a barren field, pulling up weeds. Her most tragic victim was the Thessalian hero Erysichthon.

- *Fraud*. This allegoric and infernal divinity was the incarnation of prejudice and lived in the river Cocytus, where she concealed her monstrous body that ended in a serpent's tail, so that all that could be seen was her hypocritically sweet face. She was also represented as a monster with two heads and the mask of fallacy.

- *Old Age*. The daughter of Erebus and Night, she was worshipped in both Greece and Rome. She was represented with all the traditional attributes of infirmity and sadness; dressed in black and stooped, she leaned on a stick.

19. THE LARES, THE MANES AND THE PENATES

In Roman religion, Vesta was not the only god invoked at the family hearth, for she shared this place of honour with minor gods, called the Lares, Manes and Penates. All of them were offered special veneration and sacrifices.

The Lares were the sons that Mercury had with the Naiad Lara. At first there only existed *Lar*, who was the personification of the soul of the dead, in the form of the statuette with adolescent attributes. His cult was passed from generation to generation and was meticulous and superstitious. Lar was believed to protect the Roman home. Other legends tell of twins who took their mother's name Lares and to whom the Romans offered divine respect, keeping them a space on the hearth, from where they presided over the house and home.

Their statues resembled monkeys covered in dog fur, and at their heels was a barking dog, a symbol of their care and vigilance. Later, the divinities were multiplied according to their function, for example, the domestic Lares were joined by the public Lares – which guaranteed safety on the roads, in the fields, and at crossroads – and by the city Lares – chosen from Roman gods such as Janus, Diana, and Mercury.

The *Manes* were principally guardian spirits of the home, like the Lares and the Penates. The Manes was the name generally given to the souls of the dead that previously had lived in the home. Later the name was only given to the souls of those who had been divined, and they were converted into divinities of the underworld and rendered a cult to pacify their rage. The ancestors of illustrious families were also often venerated with the name. According to some mythologists, the Manes were the children of *Mania*, Madness. However, when the people named a feared dead soul Manes, which means 'blessed', they encouraged the favours of the spirit.

The *Penates* finished the protective triad of the house and home. It is said their cult was imported from Phrygia by Tarquin the Old. However, there was a legend in Rome that tells how the Penates of the city, represented by the statues of two young men, had been brought from Troy by Aeneas. In general, the Penates presided over the house and its domestic affairs. Every head of family chose their own Penates, whom they would then invoke as special patrons. Moreover, in each home, they were reserved a place for worship and offerings, with the purpose of ensuring abundance in the home. As well as the private cults, there were the public ones that worshipped in the smallest villages and the largest cities.

The statues of the Penates were in accordance with the economic status of the family. There were Penates in ivory, clay, silver, and gold. The offerings made to them were generally a small portion of each of the family meals.

It was common among the Romans that when a family moved house, the head of the family would also take the domestic gods. Their representations were the first things to be placed in the new home, and in exchange for this gesture, the Penates blessed the family with peace and prosperity.

V. MYTHOLOGICAL COMPENDIUM

The following table may help the reader to achieve a general vision of the mythological Greek gods and their Roman counterparts, as well as being a general reference.

Greek	Roman	
Zeus	Jupiter	God of the sky, king of the gods.
Hera	Juno	Queen of the gods, protector of women.
Aphrodite	Venus	Goddess of love and beauty.
Demeter	Ceres	Goddess of fertility and the harvest.
Hestia	Vesta	Goddess of the home and the sacred fire.
Athena	Minerva	Goddess of wisdom and war.
Ares	Mars	God of war.
Hephaestus	Vulcan	God of fire.
Poseidon	Neptune	God of the sea.
Hades	Pluto	God of the Underworld.
Hermes	Mercury	The messenger god of commerce and protector of travellers.
Apollo	Apollo	God of the Sun and of prophecy.
Artemis	Diana	Goddess of hunting, the protector of animals and children.
Dionysus	Bacchus	God of wine and theatre.
Hebe	Juventas	Goddess of youth.
Eileithyia	Ilithyia	Goddess of maternity.
	Janus	God of the past and the future.
Cronus	Saturn	God of time.
Rhea	Cybele	Goddess of fertility.

FIRST GENERATION. The beginning

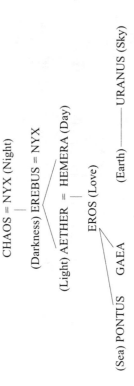

CHAOS = NYX (Night)

(Darkness) EREBUS = NYX

(Light) AETHER = HEMERA (Day)

EROS (Love)

(Sea) PONTUS   GAEA   (Earth) —— URANUS (Sky)

SECOND GENERATION. The children of Pontus and Gaea

PONTUS = GAEA

CRIUS = EURYBIA   NEREUS = DORIS   THAUMAS = ELECTRA   CETO = PHORCYS

ASTRAEUS   POSEIDON = AMPHITRITE   IRIS   THE GRAEAE AND THE GORGONS

Second generation. The Titans

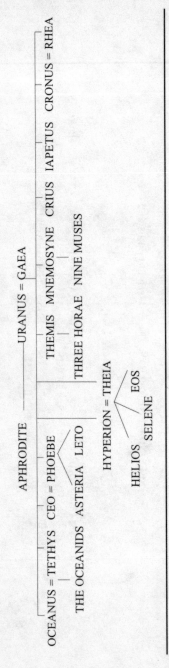

The children of Iapetus

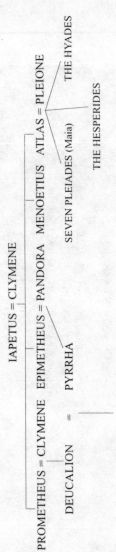

Third generation. The birth of the gods

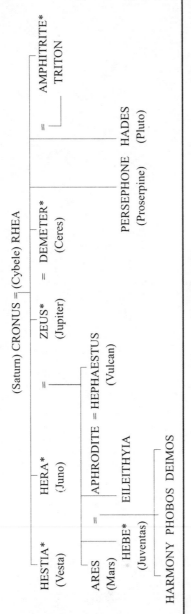

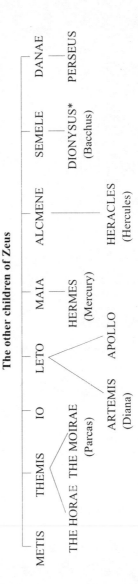

(Saturn) CRONUS = (Cybele) RHEA

HESTIA*
(Vesta)

HERA*
(Juno)

=

=

ZEUS*
(Jupiter)

= DEMETER*
(Ceres)

AMPHITRITE*

TRITON

ARES
(Mars)

APHRODITE = HEPHAESTUS
(Vulcan)

PERSEPHONE
(Proserpine)

HADES
(Pluto)

HEBE*
(Juventas)

EILEITHYIA

HARMONY PHOBOS DEIMOS

The other children of Zeus

METIS   THEMIS   IO   LETO   MAIA   ALCMENE   SEMELE   DANAE

THE HORAE THE MOIRAE
(Parcas)

HERMES
(Mercury)

APOLLO

DIONYSUS*
(Bacchus)

PERSEUS

ARTEMIS
(Diana)

HERACLES
(Hercules)

187

INDEX